The Promise of Air by Algernon Blackwood

(1913)

Algernon Blackwood was a prolific writer across short stories, novels and plays. His passion for the supernatural and for ghost stories together with a fascination for all things in the occult and mysticism created some of the most enthralling works ever written. HP Lovecraft referred to his works as that of a master. Henry James in referring to The Bright Messenger said "the most extraordinary novel on psychoanalysis, one that dwarfs the subject." Many other authors similarly lauded him. Today his works are beginning to regain their former popularity.

Index Of Contents

CHAPTER I

Joseph Wimble was the only son of an analytical chemist, who, having made considerable profits out of an Invisible Sticking Plaster, sent the boy to Charterhouse and Cambridge in the hope that he would turn out a gentleman. When Joseph left Cambridge his father left business, referred to himself as Expert, used a couple of letters after his name, and suggested making the Grand Tour of Europe together as a finishing touch. 'To talk familiarly of Rome and Vienna and Constantinople as though you knew them,' he explained, 'is a useful thing. It helps one with the women, and to be helped by women in life is half the battle.' His ambitions for his son were considerable, including above all a suitable marriage. The abrupt destruction of these ambitions, accordingly, was so bitter a disappointment that he felt justified in giving the lad a nominal sum and mentioning that he had better shift for himself. For Joseph married secretly the daughter of a Norfolk corn-chandler, announcing the news to his father upon the very eve of starting for the Grand Tour. Joseph found himself with 500 pounds and a wife.

Joseph himself was of that placid temperament to which things in life just came and went apparently without making very deep impressions. He was a careless, indifferent sort of fellow even as a boy, careless of consequences, indifferent to results: not irresponsible, yet very easy-going. There was no intensity in him; he did not realise things. 'Oh, it's much the same to me,' would be his reply to most proposals. 'I'd as soon as not.' There was something fluid in his nature that accepted life nonchalantly, as if all things were one to him; yet, again, not that he was devoid of feeling or desires, but that he did not realise life in the solid way of the majority. At school he did not realise that he was what the world calls 'not quite a gentleman,' although the boys made a point of proving it to him. At Cambridge he did not realise that to pass his Little-go, or acquire the letters B.Sc., was of any importance, although various learned and older men received good pay in order to convince him of the fact. He just went along in a loose, careless, big-hearted way of living, and took whatever came, exactly as it came. He had a delightful smile and put on fat; shared his money with one and all; existed in a methodical way as most other fellows of his age existed, and grew older much as they did. So ordinary was he in fact, so little distinguished from the rest of his kind, that men who knew him well would stop and think when questioned if they numbered Joseph Wimble among their acquaintances. 'Wimble, lemme see, oh yes, of course! Why, I've known him for a couple of years!' That was Joseph Wimble. Only it made no difference to him whether they remembered him or not. He behaved rather as if everything was one to him in a very literal sense; as if the whole bewildering kaleidoscope of life conveyed a single vast impression; there was no reason to get excited over particular details; in the end it was literally all one. His smattering of physics taught him that all things could be expressed, more or less, in terms of one another. That was his attitude, at any rate. 'Take it as a whole,' he would say vaguely, 'and it's all right. It's all the same.'

Yet his indifference to things was not so colourless as it appeared; but was due, perhaps, to the transference of his interests elsewhere. His centre of gravity hardly seemed on earth is one way of expressing it. Behind the apparent stolidity hid something that danced and sang; something almost flighty. It was laborious explanation that he dreaded and despised, as though things capable of being 'explained' were of small importance to him. He was eager to know things he wanted to know, yet in a way he was too intensely curious, too impatient certainly, to put himself to much trouble to find out. He refused to work, to 'grind' he knew not how; yet he absorbed a good deal of knowledge; information came to him, as it were. He figured to himself vaguely that there was another surer way of learning than by memorising detail, a flashing, darting, sudden way, like the way of a bird. To follow a line of information to its bitter end was a wearisome, stultifying business, the reality he sought was lost sight of in the process. The main idea had interest for him, but not the details, for the details blurred and obscured it. Proof was a stupid word that blocked his faculties. He did not despise or reject it exactly, but he refused to recognise it. In a sense he overlooked it. Of answers to the important questions millions have been asking for thousands of years there was no proof obtainable. Of survival, for instance, or the existence of the soul, there was no 'proof,' yet for that very reason he believed in both. He could 'prove' a stone, a tree, a dog. He could name and weigh and describe it. The senses of hearing, sight, and touch reported upon it, yet these reports he knew to be but vibrations of the respective nerves that brought them to his brain. They were at best indirect reports, and at worst referred to a mere collection of unverified appearances. Logic, too, the backbone of philosophy, affected him with weariness, just as his respect for reason was shockingly undeveloped. And argument could prove anything, hence argument for him was also futile. He jumped to the conclusion always. Thus at school, and even more at Cambridge, he liked to know what other fellows thought and believed, but as a whole and in outline only. A general idea of 'what and why' was enough for him, just to catch the drift.

This faculty of catching the drift of any knowledge that he cared about came to him naturally, as it seemed. They called him talented but lazy; for he took the cream off; he swooped like a bird, caught it flying, and was off upon another quest. Since there was no real proof of any of the important things, why toil to master the tedious arguments and facts of either side? There was somewhere a swifter, lighter way of knowing things, a direct and instantaneous way. He was sure of it. Thus the ordinary things of life he did not realise, quite as other people realised them. They passed him by.

One thing and one only, it seemed, he desired to realise, and that was birds. It was a passion in him, a mania. He had a yearning desire to understand the mystery of bird-life, not ornithology but birds . Anything to do with birds changed the expression of his face at once; the fat and placid indifference gave way to an emotion that, judging by his expression, caused him a degree of wonder that was almost worship, of happiness nearly painful. Their intense vitality inspired him, their equality stirred respect. Anything to do with their flight, their songs, their eggs, their habits fascinated him. And this fascination he realised. He indulged it furiously, if of necessity secretly, since to study bird-life fields and hedges must be visited without company. But here again he took no particular pains, it seemed. As is usual with an overmastering tendency, his knowledge of his subject was instinctive. Before he went to Charterhouse he knew the size and colouring of every egg that ever lay in a British nest, and by the time he left that school he could imitate with marvellous accuracy the singing notes and whistles of any bird he had heard once. He devoured books about them, studied their differing ways of flight, knew every nest within a radius of miles about his house in a given neighbourhood, and above all was moved to a kind of ecstasy of wonder over the magic of their annual migration. That in particular touched him into poetry. He thought dumbly about it, but his imagination stirred. Inarticulateness increased his accumulating store of wonder. The Grand Tour! Rome, Vienna, Constantinople, indeed! What were the capitals of Europe compared to the Southern Tour they made! That deep instinct to hurry after the fading sun, to keep in touch with their source of life, to follow colour, heat, light, and beauty. That vast autumnal flight! The marvel of the great return, entranced by the southern sun, intoxicated with the music of the southern winds! That such tiny bodies could dare four thousand miles of trackless space, travelling for the most part in the darkness, carelessly carrying nothing with them, and rush back in the spring to the very copse or hedgerow left six months before, that was a source of endless wonder to his mind. There was pathos and loneliness in their absence. England seemed empty once the birds had flown. The sky was dead without the swallows. Of course the land was dark and silent when they left, and of course it burst into colour, rhythm, movement, and singing when they showered back upon it in the spring!

The sweet passion of woodland music caught his heart. He realised that birds had a secret and mysterious life of their very own, and that the world they lived in was a happy and desirable world. That strange knowledge at a distance men called instinct, puzzled him. A new method of communication belonged to it too. It had its laws and customs, its joys and terrors, its habits, rules, and purposes; but these all were strangely different from anything that solid earth-life knew. Freedom, light, and swiftness were the characteristics of that existence, and joy its outstanding quality. Its universal telepathy exhilarated. No other beings in the universe expressed themselves naturally by singing.

The Kingdom of the Air became for him a symbol of an existence higher than anything on the earth; air stood for a condition that at present was beyond the reach of humanity, but that humanity one day would achieve. His imagination figured this glorious accomplishment as the next stage in evolution. A clever poet might have made Joseph Wimble the hero of an original fairy tale, in which he lived and suffered heavily on solid ground, eternal type of the exile, vainly yearning for his natural element, the air. For exile was in it; he claimed the knowledge of the air as a familiar experience. He felt that he knew and understood the air instinctively; he belonged 'up there'; he had nested in the trees, perched on some topmost twig, had balanced in the breeze, and sung his heart out from sheer joy of living; he had even flown.

This was doubtless a mental exercise, an imaginative flight. It all seemed familiar to him, long, long ago, before this enormous physical frame had walled him down to the ground and weight had handicapped aspiration so distressingly. He looked at his body in the glass and sighed. 'There's something wrong,' he realised. 'Why should I need such a mass of stuff to function through? I'm supposed to be more intelligent than animals or things.' He thought of a swift and sighed. Size and weight were so out of proportion to the role he played on earth. The smaller forms of life were far less handicapped; a flea, a beetle were a thousand times stronger relatively than a human being, whereas a little bird - It all left him inarticulate. He was always inarticulate. Dumbly he yearned for air; desired, that is, the mental attitude of one to whom free swift movement in the air was natural; and the intensity of the yearning, the one thing he fully realised, must some day produce a result. The beauty of an air-life hid in his blood. It expressed the ultimate yearning of his very soul.

'The next stage of the world is air,' he imagined with some part of his intelligence that never could articulately clothe the dream in language. 'We shall never be happy and right until we know the air as birds do. We've learned all the earth has got to teach us. There's a new age coming, a new element its key: Air!'

Earth, ever sweet and beautiful, was in the main, however, chiefly useful only. Somehow he no longer felt the need of it.

The unreality of objective knowledge, the limitations of the human intellect afflicted him. He thought of the barren sterility of learned minds, sacked tight with this objective information about the clothes of the universe, yet uninformed concerning the living personality that wears them. The scholars and collectors had no joy; they never sang.

He thought hard about it. He tried to state to himself what he meant in clear words. It was difficult. Already he thought in terms of air, transparent, everywhere at once, radiant and flashing. He experienced a completeness and a buoyancy that denied the accepted rule that two and two make four. Two and two, of course, did make four on earth and in the nursery or the nest. But somehow in the air, they just didn't. There was no two and two at all. They didn't exist. It was some kind of synthetical air-knowledge that he sought.

'Earth is divisible, divided,' he said to himself. 'It has details, separate objects, definite divisions into stones and things. But in the air there is no division. Air is homogeneous, not as the physicist's gas, but as an expression of space.' In the air, or rather of the air, two and two make four became not false exactly, but impossible. It could not be said. Earth is not continuous, but broken up; it belongs to time and time's divisions of the nursery. Earth is an expression of separateness. Even water has drops, fluid and cohering though it is. Air has no drops. There are no drops of air. There are currents, streams and surfaces, all undetailed. Earth, he felt, belonged to time and time's divisions where two and two made four. But air was of another category altogether, and not of time at all. Air was one.

It explained his indifference to earth. Though fastened physically like every one else to the ground, his inmost being lived in the air already, and some day he would meet a person who would explain and justify this extraordinary yearning. He was aware of this expectancy in him, for the craving to become articulate produced it. He needed a mate, of course. Together, somehow, their deep desire would find expression. He would become articulate through her. And suddenly, with a kind of abrupt surprise that belongs to birds, he found her.

The surprising way he found her, too, was characteristic. They floated, if not flew, into each other's arms.

CHAPTER II

It was a glad May morning, the air soft-flowing and cool, the sunshine warm and brilliant, when the youth cut his lectures and went out into the fields, drawn irresistibly by the electric rush and sparkle of the spring. The swallows were home from the Southern Tour, and the sky was singing. He could not sit and listen to chemical formulae in a lecture-room; it was not possible. He wandered out carelessly into the world of buttercups, following the stream where the feathered willows bent in a wave of falling green. It was a true bird-day, and his heart, uprising like the larks, was shrilling. He felt exactly like a bird himself, and it made him laugh as naturally as a bird might sing. He fell to copying their various cries. They came up close and saw him. They were aware of him. 'Birds of the sweet spring skies!' he thought, and yearned to share their strange collective life, individual still, yet part of their magical community.

He soon found himself out of the scholastic town and among the flat expanse of yellow fields beyond. The stream was blue, the grass an emerald green, the willows laughed, showing their under leaves, the dew still sparkled. Buttercups by the million nodded in the breeze; wings were everywhere, the surface of the earth was dancing, and the whole air fluttered. The earth was dressed in blue and gold.

The singing was so general that he had to pause in order to pick out the separate melodies; the song of the birds was, indeed, so much a part of their surroundings that an act of definite listening was necessary to hear it. It linked him on to Nature; it made Nature articulate. He heard the hearty whistle of the blackcap among the swaying tree-tops, shrill with joy; a whitethroat tossed itself exultantly into the air beside him; he heard the warblers trilling, the little calling cry of the chiff-chaff, the tiny poem of the willow-warbler, the merry laughter of the dainty wren. The tits shot everywhere, pecking in seed, pricking the sunshine with their tiny beaks, darting, flashing. He passed a farm and saw the vigorous outline of a blackbird, perched upon an oak bough still bare, fluting as Pan fluted upon many-fountained Ida long ago; a chaffinch dipped at him over the wall from wet shrubberies beyond, hopped to a twig in the sunlight above the blackbird, and let loose a shower of notes like silvery drops of water. Singing shook itself out of the atmosphere everywhere, as though the whole of Nature moved and trembled into her strange scale-less music. There was the joy of air upon the stirring world.

The life of air was dominant, ruling the heavy earth, bird-life. What delicious names they had, Whitethroat, Gold-oriel, Wheat-ear, Dipper, Bunting, Redpoll, Osprey, Snowy-owl, Snow-bunting, Martin; what lyrical names with fun and laughter in them, a childlike beauty of air and sunny woodland-space. The magic of Spring captured him by its suggestion: nothing was fully out, it was suggested only eternal promise, ethereal glamour: prophecy, hope, expectancy, fulfilment.

On all sides he felt the tremendous lift of the year that comes in May with song and colour and movement. The world was rhythmical. It caught him into joy, as though it would sweep him like a harp into passionate response. Yet he remained dumb and inarticulate. He drank it in: but he could not sing, he could not soar, he could not fly. This piping, fluting, thrilling, this showering stream of sweet elemental song and dance was not of the earth, but of the air. The strange yearning in him grew and gathered into a dangerous accumulation. It must find expression somehow or he would burst.

He threw himself down in the long grass beside the blue-throated stream, and became at once all eyes and ears. There was no other way. The cool touch of the luxuriant herbage brought a slight relief, as did the itemising of the songs he heard and imitated, the colours he gazed upon and named: the shimmering sheen of the rooks in the elm trees yonder; the deep, unpolished ebony of the blackbird with its beak of gleaming yellow; the bright and roving eye of the little whitethroat picking food along the bank; the shearing speed of the swifts cutting the air with tapering, scythe-like wings; the piping sweetness of a thrush, invisible in a thicket behind the farm buildings, all these combined to put the true bird-ecstasy upon him as he lay and watched and listened. The amazing outburst of spring music lifted him almost into the air to join the ropes of starlings twisting and untwisting as if they reproduced the wild soft tangle of his unsatisfied yearnings. And their tiny flickering shadows fell upon the ground in ever-shifting patterns that he could never catch or seize. Upon his mind fell similarly rushing thoughts he was unable to express . . . the rhythm of some mighty promise that uplifted. He was aware of love and beauty. The soul in him rose and twittered like a lark. . . .

Then, presently, he raised his head above the screen of grass. There was a sound of footsteps. His hearing was abnormally acute when this bird-mood took him, for the tapping tread of a wagtail on the bank had made itself distinctly heard. He saw the frisky creature, dainty as a sprite, tripping nimbly among the rushes just below him. It balanced very cleverly, neatly dressed in its tailor-made of feathers. He saw its fairy ankles. It seemed to hold its skirts up. He caught its bright eye peeping. It was gone.

'Soft, slip of a bird!' he thought to himself with a sharp sensation of regret; 'why did it leave me in such a hurry?' He felt something tender and earnest in him, something true and thorough, yet careless and light with joy, a true bird-quality. He felt, too, the pathos of the sudden disappearance: a moment ago it had been there in all its gracious beauty, and now the spot was empty.

'Where, in what new haunted corner of these fields' he began, half-singing, when a new and startling flash of loveliness caught his eye and took his breath away. Another wagtail, but this time yellow, marvellous as a dream, came pricking into view.

Somehow, beyond all understanding, the sweet apparition focussed his tangle of inarticulate yearning into a blaze of delight that was a climax. The advent of the exquisite little creature, with its delicate carriage, its bosom of pure yellow, seemed symbolical almost. The idea of something sylph-like from the heart of the air flashed into him. The whole singing, dancing, coloured element produced this living emblem from its central heart of the flooding Spring. There was true air-magic in it. The passion of Spring and the mystery of birds focussed together in the tiny symbol. Imagination touched the pitch of ecstasy. He turned abruptly. There was a whirr, a streak of burning yellow that lost itself against the sea of buttercups, and lo! He was alone again.

But this time the loneliness was more than he could bear.

He sprang to his feet, and at full speed took the direction in which it disappeared. Some wisdom of the birds was in him possibly, though alas, not their light rapidity, for while guided wisely along the windings of the willow-guarded stream, across the fields, past hedges, copses, farms, over ditches innumerable, he could not overtake his prize, and so at last came into a lonely spot that lay far away upon the surface of the countryside. The occasional flash of yellow had led him onwards in this way, as though the bird enticed him of set purpose; it would land, then shoot away again just as he came up with it. It left a trail of gold across the sunlit fields. It was a will-o'-the-wisp in sunlight. It behaved like some spiritual decoy.

Afterwards, when he thought about it, his chase took on this aspect of curious allurement, for he knew he could never catch the bird for actual handling, even had he so desired. Nor did he wish to; he had no desire to 'prove' this symbol that summed up his imaginative passion. He only wanted to come up with it; to meet its peeping eye, to watch it at close quarters: its sylph-like beauty had seduced him. Twice he dashed through the water, where the stream made a tiresome bend, and his track across the fields of early hay would have warranted a farmer in putting dust-shot into him. Yet he kept just within sight of it, of the flashing yellow which made him oblivious of all else; and the brimstone butterflies, the yellow-hammers, the orange-tinted kingfishers that obviously tried to confuse the trail by shooting across his path, failed wholly to divert him from the chase. He knew which gold to follow. It was in his heart.

The wagtail at last shot headlong past a clump of bramble-bushes, and Wimble, arriving also headlong, saw to his amazement that the yellow of its breast remained on the branches as though caught and fixed. To his astonishment the gold lay in a shining stream across the prickles without moving. It held fast. He saw the gleaming line of it. He thought he was dreaming for an instant, then discovered that the stream of gold was a yellow scarf that had been netted by the hedge. It belonged to a human being. The same second he saw a sun-bonnet and a book lying on the other side by a pond below some willows. And the being was a blue-eyed girl. His sylph of the air had come to earth. Two black stockings hung on a branch to dry. She was bare-footed. He certainly met her eye, and it was a surprised, reproachful eye. He looked down at her, and she looked up at him. His heart came up into his throat and then into his eyes.

'I suppose you know you're trespassing,' said a voice that was both cross and sweet at once. 'These fields are father's.'

'Yes,' replied young Wimble of Trinity, staring at her in amazement. 'I'm awfully sorry.' He was lost in admiration and unable to conceal it. She was more than a farmer's daughter, he was thinking, as instinctively he transferred to her all the yearning, airy passion he had put into his search for the yellow wagtail.

'Father complained last week again, and there are new boards up everywhere.' He remembered vaguely there had been complaints about trespassing; he had blundered into the very spot where the offences had been committed. 'So you've no excuse!' she added, watching him.

'I'm awfully sorry,' he repeated, as he disentangled the yellow scarf and passed the end into her outstretched hand. The sunburned skin just matched the landscape, he noted the tiny bleached hairs upon her arm. 'I saw a yellow wagtail and went after it. They're rather uncommon.' And then he added, 'I suppose it, you, got caught, scrambling through the hedge. I'm frightfully sorry. Really, I'm ashamed. I saw the bird, and forgot everything. I believe it flew back, flew into you!'

They stood looking at each other. If he cut a comical figure, she certainly did not; for whereas his face was hot, his tie flown over one shoulder, his grey trousers splashed with mud; she seemed in her natural setting between the willows and the hedge, the untidy hair falling loose about the neck, her arms akimbo and her sunburned face suiting her to perfection. She looked cool and extraordinarily radiant. He thought she was absurdly beautiful; his heart began to beat deliciously; and when she lost the cross expression and smiled at him the next moment he blurted out a confused, impetuous something before he could possibly prevent it.

'You're awfully becoming,' he stammered. 'I say, I'm jolly glad I saw that yellow wagtail and followed it. I believe it flew back into your heart.'

Her smile broadened into a laugh at once. It was impossible to be angry with such a youth. 'You undergraduates,' she said, 'are the most ridiculous people I've ever known. But I shan't let you go now I've got you. You're fairly caught.'

'Rather,' said Wimble with unfeigned delight.

'Then you'd better come with me and see father at once,' she went on. 'You can explain yourself to him, about the wagtail.'

'Rather,' he repeated, though with less enthusiasm. It was the only word that he could think of; and he added, 'presently.'

She looked him up and down. 'It's best, I think.' And her laughter was now friendly.

'I will,' he repeated, 'I'll go anywhere with you. I admit I'm caught. Do you think he'll be very nasty to me?'

But he scarcely knew what he was saying all the time, for his one desire was not to lose sight of her now that he had found her. Her face, her laughter, her singing voice, her attitude, everything about her made him gasp. He already thought of her in bird-terms. He remembered the redwing, delicate thrush, that comes to England from the North and is off again too soon, of countless birds that haunt our fields with transient beauty, then vanish suddenly, afraid to stay and rest. An anxious pang transfixed his heart. Any moment she might spread big yellow wings and leave him fluttering on the ground. 'If I've done any damage,' he added, 'I'll put it right. It was worth it, anyhow.' But he saw that she laughed with him now, not at him, and he began to smile himself. She was adorable. 'I'll swear she's a birdy girl,' the thought flashed through him.

'If you'll turn your back a moment, please,' he heard her saying, 'I'll put my shoes and stockings on again. There's no good paddling any more with you here.'

'Rather not,' he said, and ran down to fetch them for her.

And so it began and ended in the brief ten minutes of this intoxicating May morning beside the willow pond where the birds of the countryside came down to bathe at dawn and drink at sunset. It was an ideal opening. She put her stockings on, but not before he had complained that she was slow about it because a thorn had run into her toe, blaming him so that he had to extract it with trembling fingers and a penknife. They were laughing together like two children by the time he finished; and by the time they reached the house he had dipped into her being and found, as in a book of poetry, that all his favourite passages were marked. Moreover, she had led him by so round a way that they had been obliged to rest under the hedges more than once, and had discovered also that they were very hungry. The sudden intimacy was the sudden falling in love of two young persons who were obviously made for one another. It was the mating of two birds. They had met by the pond, exchanged glances, and then flown off together across the lawn. For it was spring and nesting time. . . . The dust of blue and bronze was on the dragon-flies, the bloom and promise of deep-bosomed summer in the air. . . .

'Father, this is my friend, Mr. Wimble,' she introduced him. 'You remember, I told you. He's at Trinity.'

'You'll stay and have a bite with us, won't you then? It's just time,' was the genial invitation, given to hide his excusable lack of recognition. There was no mention of the damaged fields nor of the trespassing. 'Come, Joan, let's get at it, for I'm starving.'

The name sounded wonderful, but Joseph knew it already and had already used it, his face close against her red lips and shining eyes. He also knew his fate was sealed, and he wished to heaven his own father was as nice as hers.

'I'm a chandler,' he was told in the course of the talk across the luncheon table by the window while the birds hushed their song outside, well knowing it was noon, 'a corn-chandler down in Norfolk. But I've got two farms up here in Cambridgeshire, and I'm just up to look over 'em for a chap as wants to buy 'em off me.' He was a rough-and-ready type, free in his drink and language, using meaningless oaths more frequently as intimacy grew, and betraying a somewhat irascible temperament as well. Yet he was kindly enough. And before Joseph left to go back to his forgotten lectures there had been an invitation too: 'You must come down and see us there some time if you don't mind a bit of roughing it. We live very simple.'

From all of which it was clear that the corn-chandler was favourably impressed by the visit of an Undergraduate of Cambridge University, and would not be at all averse to marrying his daughter to the first available young man with reasonable credentials. It was all so easy, instinctive, natural. It ran so smoothly. It flowed, it flew. No obstacles appeared. There was flight and rapture in it from the very start. The couple managed to see one another once a day at least for the next three weeks, but before the first week ended they were engaged. Young Wimble said nothing at home because he knew his father would object to the daughter of a corn-chandler who lived in Norfolk. By September they were married. But by the end of September Joseph realised that they were married, quite another thing. For his father meant what he said, and beyond a modest allowance from the chandler to his daughter, they started life with nothing but the small lump sum by means of which Mr. Wimble senior eased his conscience and set himself right with the outside world. The capitals of Europe were not visited.

Joseph and Joan, however, took the situation like a pair of birds, lightly and carelessly. They were as thoughtless as two finches on the lawn, and as faithful as red linnets. The game of the yellow wagtail chase was kept up between them. He pretended that it was her flying scarf he had seen shining two miles across the buttercup fields, and she declared that she had gone to the willow pond on purpose, knowing in her bones, she called them feathers, that one day some one would find her there and capture her. The actual wagtail was a real decoy. It was his yearning and her own materialised.

They laughed and played with the idea till it grew very real. And the future did not frighten them a bit. They took their money and spent it on their honeymoon, leaving for the south in October with the birds. They started on the great Southern Tour, building their first nest far away in a sun-drenched Algerian garden where the air, soft with the bloom of an eternal summer, mastered the earth and made it seem of small account. Nothing could weigh them down, nor cage them in. They led a true air-life together, the winds were softly scented, stars shone nightly above their cosy tent, they sang in the golden sunsets and washed their young bodies in the morning dew.

It was the paradise of a realised dream, a sparkling ecstasy they thought could never end. Her beauty seemed to him the one thing necessary. The autumn migration of the birds, mysterious with grandeur, had always suggested to him a passing-away from earth, a procession to another life, and a returning to sing of it with rapture in the spring. Their honeymoon was this dream come true.

They mated and married as birds do, on the wing, and singing. And their first-born, a girl, was the offspring of a passion as intense and radiant as any passion can be in this world. Their imaginative ecstasy, prolonged wondrously through golden months, lifted them from the earth towards the very stars. In it was singing, flight, and rapture, the freedom of wild free spaces and the glory of flashing, coloured wings.

It was of the air. They fluted to one another beneath the moon; they soared above the noonday heat, they warbled in the scented dusk. Their child, conceived of sun and wind, in a transport of bliss akin to that careless passionate happiness that makes bird-life a ceaseless running song, was born where the missel-thrush sings in the moonlight, and the nightingales in February. She was a veritable child of air. A bird on the wing dropped her to earth in passing, and was gone. . . .

But something else was gone about that time as well. There came the collapse of inevitable reaction, tragedy. It was as pitiful as anything well could be. Having accomplished her chief end in life, the wife's strange beauty faded: her lightness, brilliance waned, her rapture sank and died; she became a heavy, rather stupid mother; she returned to type whence youth and imagination had temporarily rescued her. Her underlying traits of ordinary texture dulled the colour of her yellow wings. She bequeathed her all to this radiant, sparkling firstborn, and herself went out. The thing he loved in her vanished or became obliterated. He had caught her main drift; he tired. She tired too. In him patient affection replaced ecstatic adoration; in her there was tolerance, misunderstanding, then disappointment. To live longer on the heights they had first climbed became impossible. All that had fascinated him, caught him into the air, departed from her. The bird flew from her into the little girl with yellow hair and big blue eyes.

She wearied of the life in tents and spoke of 'artistic furniture' at home, of comfort, and began to wonder how their 'living' could be 'earned.' The practical outlook developed, the carelessness of air decreased. Tom, the second-born, was the culminating proof of the saddening descent. He was just a jolly little dirty animal. 'He's like a rabbit,' thought his father, looking with disappointment on him, thus introducing the big, bitter quarrel that ended in their coming back to the heavy skies of England, settling in a flat in Maida Vale, and led eventually to his taking up work in connection with a modern publishing house to provide the necessary food and rent and clothing. They landed with a distinctly heavy thud on earth.

It was, on the mother's part, a great tragedy of sacrifice. Having given all her best qualities to the first-born, she kept none over for herself, not even enough to appreciate her loss. Her radiance, sparkle, lightness, all her airy wonder, joy and singing, passed from her into yellow-haired little Joan. She stared at it with dull misunderstanding in her heart. She had not retained enough even to understand herself. She did not even discover that she had changed, for only when a fragment remains is the loss of the rest recognised, much less regretted.

By expressing herself in reproduction, she had not grown richer, but had somehow merely emptied herself. Her husband, moreover, was not heartless. He was not even to blame. He remained tender, kind, and true, but he did not love. For the thing he loved had gone into another form.

Like the shifting shadows of the wings upon the Cambridge flats that gay spring morning, there fell upon his mind a shower of vague and indescribable thoughts, only one of which he pounced upon before it fled away.

'What has been so long unconscious in me, little Joan may perhaps make conscious. I wonder . . .!' He wondered till he died. He kept his wings, that is.

CHAPTER III

The return to London was a return to the demands of earth; from the bright and fiery aether of the southern climate they landed with something of a jar among sooty bricks and black-edged mortar. The sunshine dimmed, the very air seemed solid. Regular hours of work made it difficult for him to lift his wings, much less to fly; he knew the London air was good, but he never noticed that it was air at all; he almost forgot they had ever lived in the air and flown at all. Grocers, butchers, and bakers taught Mrs. Wimble to become very practical, and the halfpenny newspapers stirred her social ambitions for her children. Wimble worked hard and capably, and they made both ends meet. He proved a patient husband and a devoted father, if perhaps a rather vague one. His moment of realisation was over. He accepted the routine of the majority, living methodically, almost automatically, yet always a little absent-mindedly as though much of his intelligence was unconsciously at work elsewhere.

Both parents altered; but, whereas his change was on the surface only, his wife's seemed fundamental and permanent. He was aware that he had altered, she was not aware. They differed radically, for instance, about the prolonged and golden honeymoon in the south.

'The money lasted uncommonly well,' said Mrs. Wimble when they spoke of it; 'it was a pity we didn't keep over a little, wasn't it?' There was a hint of asperity in the droop of her lips.

'We should have it now if we had,' he answered vaguely but with patience. 'But for me it's a memory that will always live.' He spoke with longing tenderness.

'What?' said Mrs. Wimble, who, like all slow thinkers, liked sentences repeated, thus giving time to find an intelligent reply.

'We had a lovely time out there,' she admitted with a sigh, and went on to mention by way of complaint that she feared she was getting rather stout in London. There was no idea in her that she had changed in any other way; she looked back upon Algeria as a kind of youthful madness, half regretting it. That the bird had flown from her heart did not occur to her. Not alone her body, but her mind was getting stout. She had grown so artificial that she was no longer real. The manners, moods, the words and gestures she adopted in order to please or in order to appear as others are, had ended by effectually screening her own natural self, that which is every one's possession of unique value. It was not so much that she was false as that she was not herself. She was unreal.

In Wimble, however, those two years remained as something bewilderingly beautiful. Just out of sight in his heart he wore still the steady glow of it. He never could recall quite what he had felt in those deliriously happy days, yet the knowledge that they had been deliriously happy remained and warmed his blood. It was a big, brave, heartening memory beneath his coloured waistcoat. He dreamed his dream, only he did not tell it to any one yet. He remained a kind, untidy husband and father. But that was the outer portion of him. The inner portion flew and soared and even sang. He no longer quite understood the meaning of this inner portion, but some day, he felt, it would be drawn out of him again and recognised. He would be taught to realise it, and what this bird-thing in him meant would be made clear. Already he looked to little Joan with something more than an infatuated father's adoration for her yellow hair, her bright blue eyes, her light and dancing ways.

Tom he just loved in the way his mother loved. He remained a rabbit with distinctive tendencies of the animal. But with Joan it was different. In Joan there was something he looked forward to. Even at the age of five there was a glint about her that increased the glow in him; at ten it was still more marked. She puzzled her mother considerably, just as later she alarmed her. 'I'm nervous about the child; she doesn't seem like other girls of her age. I don't see her getting on much,' was her opinion, expressed again and again in the same or similar language. 'Joan seems to me backward.'

'Well,' admitted her husband, 'she's certainly not in a hurry about it. She's maturing slowly. Lots of them do, when there's a good deal to mature.'

'I hope you're right, Joe.' And then she added with pride by way of compensation, 'Tom's coming along nicely, anyhow,' as though she spoke of a growing vegetable or, as he thought, of a rabbit in a cage with lettuces in front of it, and the idea of mating the chief end in life.

Once past the age of sixteen, however, Joan too came along nicely, and with a sudden rush that reminded her father of a young bird consciously leaving the nest. She seemed to mature so abruptly. There came a wondrous bloom upon her, as though the South poured up and blossomed in her body, mind, and soul. It took her father deliciously by surprise. The glowing thing in him spread too, rose to the surface, caught fire. He watched her with amazement, joy, and pride. He felt wings inside him. Thought danced, flashed against a background of blue and gold again.

'She'll do something in the world before she's done,' he said confusedly to himself, feeling a prophecy he had always made without realising it. 'There's wings in the girl. She'll teach them how to fly!'

He was beginning to realise himself through her. His early ideal had taken flesh again, but this time with a difference. He had not merely found it. He had created it.

For, more and more lately, the influence of Joan upon him had been growing. It was not merely that she made him feel young again, nor that her queer ways made him aware that he wanted to sing and dance. It was, in a word, that he recognised in her the remarkable thing he had known first in her mother years ago, but released in all its golden fullness. He recovered in her sparkling presence the imaginative dream that had caught him up into the air in youth, and it was both in her general attitude to life as well as in the odd things she now began to say and do. Her general attitude expressed it better than her words and acts. She was it, lived it naturally. She had the Air in her. In her presence the old magic rose over him again. He remembered the strange boyhood's point of view about it, that a new thing was stealing down into the world of men, a new point of view, a new way of looking at old, dull, heavy things, that Air was catching at the heart of humanity here and there, trying to lift it somehow into freedom. He thought of the collective wisdom and brotherhood of birds. He forgot that he was growing old.

The old longing for carelessness, lightness, speed in life, these snatched at him with passionate yearning once again. Joan was the air-idea personified. And she had begun to find herself.

But so long now had he lived the mole-existence in London that at first this delicious revival baffled and bewildered him. He could not suddenly acquire speed without the risk of losing balance.

He became aware of a maddening desire to escape. He wanted air. Joan, he felt positive, knew the way. But the majority of people about him, his wife, Tom, their visitors, their neighbours, had not the least idea what it was he meant. And this lack of comprehension gave him a feeling of insecurity. He was out of touch with his environment. He was above, beyond, in advance of it. He was in the air a little.

He looked down on them in one sense.

There were times when he did not know whether he was standing on his head or his feet. 'Everything looks different suddenly,' as he expressed it. He saw things upside down, or inside out, or backwards forwards. And the condition first betrayed itself one afternoon when he returned unexpectedly from work, he was still traveller to a publishing house, and found his wife talking over the tea-cups with a caller. He burst into the room before he knew that any one was there, and did not know how to escape without appearing rude. He sat down and fingered a cup of tea. They were talking of many things, the sins of their neighbours in Maida Vale, chiefly, and after the pause and interruption caused by his unwelcome entrance, the caller, searching for a suitable subject, asked:

'You've heard about Captain Fox, I suppose?'

'What?' asked Mrs. Wimble, opening her eyes as though anxious to read the other's thoughts. Evidently she had not heard about Captain Fox.

'I don't think I have,' she said cautiously. 'What in particular?'

'He's going to marry her,' was the reply. 'I know it for a fact. But don't say anything about it yet, because I heard it from Lady Spears, who . . .'

She dragged a good deal of Burke into the complicated explanation, making it as impressive as she could. Captain Fox, who was no better than he should be, according to the speakers, paid rather frequent visits upon the young widow of the ground-floor flat, who should have been better than she was. To find that honest courtship explained the friendship was something of a disappointment. Mrs. Marks wished to be the first to announce the innocent interpretation, to claim authorship, indeed, having persistently advocated the darker view.

'Who'd ever have guessed that?' exclaimed Mrs. Wimble, off her guard a moment. 'You always told me -'

The face of her caller betrayed a passing flush.

'Oh, one always hoped,' she began primly, when Mrs. Wimble interrupted her with a firm, clear question:

'By the bye, who was she?' she asked.

And hearing it, Wimble felt his world turn upside down a moment. He realised, that is, that his wife saw it upside down. For his wife to ask such a question was as if he had asked it himself. He felt ashamed. His world turned inside out. He looked down on them. He rose abruptly, finding the energy to invent a true-escaping sentence:

'You ask who she was,' he said, not with intentional rudeness, yet firmly, 'when you ought to ask'

Both ladies stared at him with surprise, waiting for him to finish. He was picking up the cup his sudden gesture had overturned.

'Who she is,' concluded Wimble, with the astonishment of positive rebuke in his tone. 'What can it matter who she was? It's what she is that's of importance. The Captain's got to live with that.' And then the escaping-sentence: 'If you'll excuse me, Mrs. Marks, I have to go upstairs to see a book', he hesitated, stammered, and ended in confusion 'about a book.' And off he went, making a formal little bow at the door. He went into the dining-room down the passage, vaguely aware that he had not behaved very nicely. 'But, of course, I'm not a gentleman exactly,' he said to himself; 'what's called a gentleman, that is. Father was only an analytical chemist.'

He stood still a moment, then dropped into a chair beside the table with the red and black check cloth. His mind worked on by itself, as it were.

'What I said was true, anyhow. People always ask, "Who was she?" about everything. What the devil does that matter? It's what you are that counts. Father was a chemist, but I, I -'

He got up and walked over to the clock, because the clock stood on the mantelpiece, and there was a mirror behind it. He wanted to see his own face. He stared at himself a moment without speaking, thinking, or feeling anything. He put his tie straight and picked a bit of cotton from his shoulder.

'I am Joseph Wimble, not a gentleman quite, not of much account anywhere perhaps, but a true workman, earning 250 pounds a year, knowing all about the outside, and something about the inside of books; thirty-seven years old, with a boy at the Grammar School, a girl of sixteen in the house, and married to, to -' He paused, turned from the mirror, and sat down. It cost him an effort to remember, 'to Joan Lumley, daughter of a corn-chandler in Norfolk, who might die any moment and leave us enough to live on,' he went on, 'in a more comfortable position,' passing his hand over his forehead; 'and my life is insured, and I've put a bit by, and Tom's to be a solicitor's clerk, and everything's going smoothly except that taxes -'

The sound of an opening door disturbed him. He felt confused in his mind. He heard Mrs. Marks saying loudly, 'And please say good-bye for me to your husband,' the aspirate so emphasised that it was obviously an insecurity. She intended he should hear and understand she bore him no ill-will for his bad manners, yet despised him. The steps went downstairs, and the two questions came back upon him like pistol-shots:

'Who was she? Who am I?

He realised he had been wandering from the point.

'I'm a centre of life, independent and unafraid,' thought flashed an answer. 'I'm what I make myself, what I think myself. I'm not seeing things upside down; I'm beginning to think for myself, and that's what it is. No one, nor nothing, nor anything anywhere in the world,' he went on, mixed in speech, but clear in mind, 'can prevent me from being anything I feel myself, will myself, say I am. I've never read nor thought nor bothered my head about things before. By heavens! I'll begin! I have begun -'

'What's the matter, Joe? Have you got a headache, or is it the books bothering you, dear?' His wife had come in upon him.

She put her hand upon his forehead, and he got up from his chair and faced her.

'I've made a discovery,' he said, with exhilaration in his manner, 'a great discovery.' He looked triumphantly at her. 'I am.'

'What are you?' she asked, thinking he was joking, and his sentence left unfinished on purpose.

'I am,' he repeated with emphasis. 'I have discovered that I am, that I exist. Your question to that woman made me suddenly see it.'

His wife looked flustered, and said vaguely, 'What?' Wimble continued:

'As yet, I don't know exactly what I am, but I mean to find out. Up till now I've been automatic, just doing things because other people do 'em. But I've discovered that's not necessary. I'm going to do things in future because I want to. But first I must find out why I am what I am. Then the explanation'll come of everything. Do you see what I mean? It's a case of "Enquire within upon everything."' And he smiled. His heart fluttered. He felt wings in it again.

'Do you mean you're going to start in the writing or publishing line, Joe?' It had always been her secret ambition.

'That may come later,' he told her, 'when I've something to say. For it's really big, this discovery of mine. Most people never find it out at all. She', indicating with his thumb the direction Mrs. Marks had taken, 'hasn't, for instance. She simply isn't aware that she exists. She isn't.'

'Isn't what, dear?'

'She is not, I mean, because she doesn't know she is,' he said loudly.

'Oh, that way. I see.' Mrs. Wimble looked a wee bit frightened. He had seen an animal, a rabbit for instance, look like that before it decided to plunge back into its hole for safety.

'There are strange, big things about these days, I know,' she said after a pause, thinking of the books with queer titles his employers published. 'You have been reading too much, dear, thinking and -'

'Mother,' he interrupted, instinctively omitting her name, and in a tone that convinced her his head was momentarily turned, 'that's the whole trouble. I've never thought in my life.'

'But why should you, dear?' she soothed him, wondering if people who lost their memory and wandered off exhibited such symptoms first. 'You always do your work splendidly. Don't think too much, is what I say. It always leads to worrying'

'Hardly ever, till this moment,' he was saying in the grave, emphatic way that so alarmed her. 'Not even when I asked you to marry me, when Tom was born, or Joan, or when we took this flat, or anything.'

'You've made quite a success of your life without it anyhow, Joe dear. And no woman could ask more than that. D'you feel poorly? Joan can fetch Dr. Monson in a moment.' It was a variant of 'What?'

'I feel better and bigger and stronger,' he replied, 'more real than ever in my life before. I have never been really alive till this moment. I am, and for the first time I know it. I'm experiencing.' He stopped short, as Joan went down the passage singing, pausing a moment to look in, then tactfully going on her way again. The fluttering in his heart became more marked. Something was trying to escape. There was a whirr of wings again. 'Mother,' he said to his wife, as their heads turned back from the door together, 'do you know what "experiencing" is? D'you realise what the word means?'

She sat down, resting her arms upon the table. She looked quietly into his eyes, as at one who is about to speak out of greater knowledge.

'Joe dear, I have had experiences, experiences of my very own, you know.'

'Yes, yes, I know, I know. But what I mean is, do you get the meaning, the real meaning of the word?'

She sighed audibly. 'Not your meaning, perhaps,' she meant. But she did not say it.

'It means,' he said, delighted with her exquisite silence, 'it means, er' He thought hard a moment. 'Experience,' he went on, 'is that "something" which changes potatoes into nourishment, and so into emotion. That's it. Until you eat potatoes, you don't exist. Until you have experiences, you don't exist. When you have experiences and know that you have them, you persist.'

She gasped aloud. She took his hand, very quietly.

'Joe dear,' she said, softly as in their courtship days, 'such ideas don't come into your head from nowhere. Has some one been talking to you? Have you been reading these books?'

His pulse was very quiet.

'Have you been reading the firm's books, dear?' she repeated.

She asked it gently, forgivingly, as a mother might ask her boy, 'Have you been tasting father's whisky?' The books were meant to sell to booksellers, to the public, to people who needed that particular kind of excitement. Her husband was to be trusted. He was not supposed to know what they contained. His 'line' of trade was chiefly medical, psychological, religious, philosophical. Fiction was another 'line', for the apprentice. Joe was an 'expert' traveller. He was expected to talk about his wares, but not as one who read them. Merely their selling value was his strong point.

By the expression of his face she knew the answer.

He leaned back in his chair, just as he did sometimes when he asked what there was for dinner, the same real interest in his eyes, and he answered very calmly:

'My dear, I have a bit. Cogito ergo sum. For the first time I understood, in theory, that I existed. My reading taught me that. But I never knew it in practice until just now, when I heard you ask that question about the future Mrs. Fox: "Who was she?" And then I knew also that you -'

'You what?' enquired Mrs. Wimble, bridling.

'Were unaware that you existed,' he replied point blank.

'Aren't you a little beside yourself, Joe, sort of excited, or something? 'she gasped, proud of her tact and self-control. 'What else could I have said? How could I have put it different?'

'Joan,' he answered gently, 'you should have said, "What is she?" For that would have meant you thought for yourself. It would have meant that you knew you were, and that you knew she was.'

'Original?' said Mrs. Wimble slowly, catching her husband's meaning vaguely, but more than a little disturbed in her mind.

'No,' he answered, 'true. Just as when, years ago, the sunshine lovely and the fields full of buttercups, you wore a yellow scarf, and a wagtail beside a willow pond came so near that -'

'Joe,' she said with a slight flush that was half displeasure yet half flattered vanity,' you needn't bring up that again. We were a bit above ourselves, dear, when that happened. We lost our heads'

'Above ourselves! Free and real and happy,' he interrupted her, 'that's what we were then. We had wings. We've lost 'em. We were in the air, I tell you.' His voice grew louder. 'And what's more, we knew it.'

He heard his daughter pass down the narrow passage again, singing. He got up and seemed to shake himself. There was again a fluttering in him.

'We certainly were in the air,' murmured his astonished wife.

'You were a glorious yellow wagtail,' he went on, so that she didn't know whether his laughter was in earnest or in play, 'and we were rising into flight. We've come down to earth since. We live in a hole, as it were. I'm going to get out!'

Joan's little song went past the door and died away towards the kitchen:

Flow, fly, flow,   Wherever I am, I go.

'We've lost our wings. We crawl about. We never dance now, or sing, or -' He broke off abruptly. He felt the other portion of himself, so long hidden, coming to the surface; and he was aware that it went after his daughter. He was a little afraid of it, felt giddy. Her voice in the distance sounded like a lark's, the lilt of her curious little song had an echo of the open air in it, her tread brought back the tripping of the wagtail along the river's bank. 'We never get out now,' he finished the sentence, 'we never get out. Earth smothers us. We want air!'

Mrs. Wimble watched him a moment with frightened eyes. He was standing on tiptoe, holding the tails of his coat in his hands as though he was about to do something very unusual, something foolish and ridiculous, she thought. He seemed about to dance, to rise, almost to fly up to the ceiling. She felt uneasy, hot, a little ashamed.

'We can go out more, dear, if you think it wise,' she said cautiously, moving a little further away. 'It's the expense, I always thought -'

Her husband stared at her a moment dumbly. He seemed to be listening. In his heart a little, forgotten song crept back, answering the singing of the girl. Then, dropping upon his heels again, he said patiently in a soothing tone:

'There, there, Mother! Forgive me if I frightened you. I was only pretending we were young again. That old bird thing, bird-magic, came over me for a moment. The girl's singing did it, I suppose. Something ageless in me got the upper hand . . .'

He took her hand and comforted her. 'Steady, Joe,' she said, horribly puzzled, 'she is a bit flighty, I know.'

'But we will go out more,' he went on more normally again, adopting her meaning perfectly. 'Bother the expense! We'll go out this very night and take the child with us. We'll dine out, my dear. I'll take you to a West End restaurant!'

CHAPTER IV

For Joan certainly was no ordinary girl; some called her backward, some considered her deficient, but all agreed that she was singular. Yet all liked her. Tall, slim and fair, with plenty of golden hair and eyes of merry brightness, she was out of the common in an attractive sort of way. Tom, her brother, with the mind of a solicitor's clerk, looked down upon her; her mother, fond, conventional, socially ambitious, despaired of her; her father alone held the opinion, 'There's something in that girl. She's always herself. But town-life over-weights and hides her; and in the end will suffocate. It'll snuff her out. She's meant for country.' He was aware of something unusually real in her. They were great friends. 'I want more air,' she had said once. 'In a field or garden I'd grow enormous like a bean plant. In these streets I'm just a stone squashed down by crowds. I'm in a hole and can't breathe. I prefer a fewity.' Even her words were her own like this. 'I'd like room to dance in. Life is a dance. I'd learn it in a field. I'd be a bird girl.' Space was her need, for mind as well as body.

It was her father's secret ambition too: a cottage, a garden with things that grew silently into beauty, flowers, vegetables, plants; sweet laughing winds; the rush of living rain at midnight; water to drink from a deep, cool spring instead of from metal pipes; a large, inviting horizon in which a man might lose himself; and above all, birds.

'After a month in real private country, loose country, talking, dancing, running country' She paused.

'Liquid, fluid, as it were,' he put in, delighted.

'Yes, deep and clear as a river,' she went on, 'in country like that, do you know what'd happen to me, father, after a few months of waiting?'

'I know, but I can't quite say,' he answered. 'Tell me, child, for I'd love to hear your own description.'

'I'd fly,' was her answer. 'Everything in me would fly about like a bird, picking up things, and all over the place at once without a plan, a fixed, heavy plan like a street or square in London here, and yet getting on all the time, getting further.'

'And how would you learn, dear?'

'Birds,' she laughed. 'There's bird-teaching, I'm sure.' She flitted across to another chair as she said it. She came closer to her father, who was listening with both ears, watching, drinking in something he had known long ago and then forgotten. 'You know all about it, Daddy. You needn't pretend.'

'You're rather like one, d'you know,' he smiled. 'Like a bird, I mean.' He thought of a dabchick that hides so cleverly no one can put it up, then, suddenly, is there, close at hand.

She was perched on his knee before he knew it. Her small voice twittered on into his ear. Something about her sparkled, flashed and vanished, and it reminded him of sunshine on swift-fluttering wings through the speckled shade of an orchard. She darted, whirred, and came to rest. He stroked her.

'Father, you know everything before I say it,' she went on, her face shining with happiness that made her almost beautiful. 'If I could only live like a bird, I could live. Here it's all a big, stuffy cage.' She flitted to the window, pointing to roofs and walls and chimney-pots, black with grime. The same instant she was back again upon his knees. 'To live like a bird is to be alive all over, I'm sure, I'm sure. I know it. It's all routing here.'

Whether she meant rotten, routine, or living in a rut, he did not ask. He felt her meaning.

'There's a nest in a garden waiting for us somewhere,' he said, living the dream with her in his heart. 'And it's got an orchard, high deep grass, wild flowers, hills in the distance, with a tremendous sky where the winds go tearing about like the flight of birds. And a stream that ripples and sings and shines. All alive, I mean, and always moving. They say the country's stagnation. It isn't. It's a perfect rush'

'Of course,' she put in. 'Oh, father, think hard about that place, and we'll attract it nearer and nearer, till in the end we drop into it and grow like -'

'Beans,' he laughed.

'Birds,' she rippled, and hopped from his knee across the room, and was down the passage and out of sight before he could draw another breath.

There was something alert as lightning in the girl. She woke a similar thing in him, too. It had nothing to do with brain as intellect, or with reason, or with knowledge in the ordinary sense the world gives to these words. But it had to do, he dimly felt, with another bigger thing that was everywhere and in everything. Joan shared it, brought it nearer; it was universal. What that bigger thing might be perplexed him. He was aware that it drove past, alertness in so huge a thing conveying the impression of vast power. There was grandeur in it somewhere, poise, dignity, beauty; yet this subtle alertness too, and this swift protean sparkle. It was towering as a night of stars, alluring as a peeping wildflower, but prodigious also as though all the oceans flowed suddenly between narrow banks in a flood of clearest water, very rapid, terrifyingly deep. For a robe it wore the lustrous colouring of untold age. His imagery, when he tried to visualise it, grew mixed. He called it Experience. But sometimes he told himself he knew its Christian name, its familiar, little, intimate nickname, and that was Wisdom.

And so he was rather glad that Joan, like himself, was but half educated; that she was backward, and that he knew, relatively, only the outsides of books. For facts, he vaguely felt, might come between them and this august yet precious thing they knew together. Birds could teach it, but Ornithology hid it.

Lately, however, as his wife divined, he had been dipping in between the covers of the goods he travelled in. Caught by the bait of several drugging titles, he had nibbled, in the train, in waiting-rooms, in the 'parlours' of commercial hotels where he put up for the night. He had found names and descriptions of various things, but they were the names and descriptions given by others to their own sensations. The ordered classification merely developed snapshots. He recognised photographs of dead things that he knew must be somewhere alive. The names made stationary what ought to dance along with incessant movement. Only he did not realise this until he saw the photographs. The alleged accuracy of a photograph was an insolent falsehood, pretending that what was alive was dead, that what rushed was stationary. Dogs and savages cannot recognise the photographs of their masters. The resemblance has to be taught. Everything flows, his shilling Heraclitus told him. He had always known it. Birds taught it. Joan lived it. To classify was to photograph, a prevarication. To publish a snapshot of a jumping horse was to teach what is not true. Definitions were trivial and absurd, for what was true to-day was false to-morrow. The sole value of names, of classification, of photographing lay in stopping life for an instant so that its flow might be realised, as a momentary stage in an incessant process. And he looked at a group of acquaintances his wife had 'Kodaked' ten days ago, and realised with delight how they all had rushed away, torn on ahead, lived, since she had told that insignificant lie in black and white about them.

Joan, catching him in the act of destroying it, had said, 'I know why you're doing that, father.'

'Why?' he asked, half ashamed and half surprised.

'Because you don't want to stop them,' was her answer, 'and because it wasn't fair of mother to catch them in the act like that. It wasn't all.'

And as he stared at her curious peeping face, she came quickly up to him, saying passionately, imploringly:

'Oh, do let's get into the country soon, and live along with it, and grow and know things. I feel so stuck still here, and always caught-in-the-act like that photo. It's so dead. It's a toad of a place! The streets are all nailed down on to the ground. In the country they run about'

He interrupted her on purpose:

'But in a city life is supposed to be much richer than in the country,' he said. 'You know that?'

'It goes round and round like a circle, though; it doesn't go on. I'm living other people's lives here. I want to live my own. Everybody here lives the same thing over and over again till they get so hot they get ill. I want to be cool and naked like a fern. Here I'm being photographed all day long. Every man who looks at me takes a photograph. Oh, father, I'm so tired of it. Do let's go soon and live hoppily like the birds.'

'You mean happily?' he asked, laughing with her.

'It's the same thing,' she laughed back, 'it's like wings or running water, always going wherever they are

    Flow, fly, flow,   Wher-ev-er I am I go   I live on the run,   Like a bird that's fun!   Flow, fly, flow . . .

And was dancing to and fro over the carpet, when the door opened and in came her brother Tom, followed by another youth.

He looked surprised, ashamed, then vexed. It was Saturday afternoon. He had been six months now in the office.

'I've brought Mr. Halliday with me,' he said pompously, 'to have tea. We've just been to a matinee at the Coliseum. Joan, this is Mr. Halliday, our junior clerk. My sister, Harold.'

Joan instantly looked gauche and ugly. She shook hands with a speckled youth, whose shy want of manners did not prevent his eyeing her all over. He sat down beside his friend, talking of the singing, dancing, juggling and so on that they had witnessed. All the time he talked at something else in her. But she hid it away as cleverly as a bird hides its nest. The callow youth, without realising it, was hunting for a nest. In the country he might have found it. He would have been sunburned, for one thing, instead of speckled. The wind, the rain, the starlight would have guided him. His natural instinct would have flowed out in a dance of spontaneous running movement, easy, graceful, clean. Here, however, it seemed rigid, ugly, diseased. He was living the life of others.

'You were dancing just as we came in,' observed Mr. Halliday. 'Does that line of things attract you? You are going on the stage, perhaps?'

Joan looked past him out of the window, and saw the swallows flashing about the sky.

'I can dance,' she replied, 'but not on a stage.'

'But you'd be a great success, I think, from what I saw,' opined the junior clerk. And somehow he said it unpleasantly. His tone half undressed her.

She didn't flush, she didn't stammer, at first she didn't answer even. She watched the swallows a moment, as though she had not heard him.

'You only stare, you don't watch and enjoy,' she said suddenly, turning upon him. 'And an audience like that. . .!' She stopped, got up from her chair, put her head out of the open window and gazed into the air above. When she turned back, she saw that her mother had come in and was leading the others into the dining-room for tea. Her father's face wore a singular expression, it seemed, of exultation. Tom, black as a thunder-cloud, waited for her.

'You're nothing but a little barbarian,' he said angrily under his breath. The life of others he led had been sorely wounded. 'I can never bring Mr. Halliday here again. You're simply not a lady.'

'I'm a bird,' she laughed in his face. 'And you men can never understand that, because no man has a bird in him, but only a creepy, crawly animal. We go on two legs, you on four.'

'I'm ashamed of you, Joan. You're nothing but a savage.' He snapped at her. He could have smacked her. His face was flushed, but his neck thin, scraggy, white. He looked starved and twisted. 'In the City we' he began with a clown's dignity.

'Live like rats in a drain,' she interrupted quickly, perched a moment on her toes in front of his face. 'You don't breathe or dance. Tom,' she added with a gesture of her arms like flapping wings, 'if you were alive, you'd be a mole. But you're not. You're a lot of other people. You're a herd, always enclosed and always feeding.'

She danced down the corridor and into her room, locked the door, slipped out of some tight clothing, and began to sing her bird-song of incessant movement:

   Flow! Fly! Flow!   Wherever I am I go;   I live on the run   Like the birds it's fun!   Flow, fly, flow. . . .

She sang it to a tiny, uneven, twittering melody that was made up of half notes. It went on and on, repeating itself without end. It seemed to have no real end at all.

CHAPTER V

To others she was doubtless an exasperating being. To her father alone, since he saw in her something he had lost but was now recovering, something he therefore idealised, seeing in perfected form what was actually but a germ still, to her father she expressed a little of that higher carelessness, or wisdom, that he had touched in boyhood and now yearningly desired again.

'Oh, she's all in the air,' people said. And it was truer than they knew. She had an affinity with all that flew. This bird-idea was in her heart and blood. Whatever flew, whatever rose above the ground, whatever passed swiftly, suddenly, from place to place, without deliberation, without calculation, without weighing risk and profit, this appealed to her. Yet there must be steadiness in it somewhere too, and it must get somewhere. A swallow or a butterfly she approved, but not a bat. The latter, for all its darting swiftness, was a sham; it was an earth-crawler really, frightened into ridiculous movement by finding itself aloft like a blown leaf; like a flying fish, it was wrong and out of place. It merely flew round and round in stupid, broken circles without rhythm. But the former were perfect. They were ideal. They were almost spirits.

And when her father said he was glad she was half educated, he only meant glad that she had left school and teachers before her butterfly mind had become a rigid, accurate, mechanical thing. She might play with books as he himself did, fluttering over the covers, smelling their perfume, glancing at sentences and chapter headings, at indices even. But she must not build nests in them. A book, like a photograph, was an evillish attempt to nail a flowing idea into a fixed pattern. In the author's mind an idea was true, but when he had put it down in black and white he had put down only a snapshot of it: the idea was already far away.

'Not poetry-books,' Joan qualified this, 'because poetry runs clean off the page. It's alive and wingy. It sings my bird-song

    Flow, fly, flow,   Wherever I am I go!

She had this unerring instinct of the bird in everything, the quality that flashes, darts, is gone before it can be killed by capture. A bird is everywhere and nowhere. It's all over the place at once. Look at it, and it's no longer there; listen to it, and it's gone; touch it, and you catch a sunbeam that warms the hand but loses half its beauty; catch it and it's dead. But no one ever caught a swallow or a skylark naturally on the wing. Even the eye, the mind, the following thought grows dizzy in the effort.

For the cow in the field she had no song. 'Wherever I am, I stay,' was without a tune of its own. A cow couldn't leave the ground. She wanted something with incessant movement that could touch the earth, yet leave it at will. Wings and water could. Birds and rain both flew. Half the time a river (the only real water for her) flowed over the earth without stopping on it, and half the time it was a cloud in the sky, yet never lived there. 'Flow, fly, flow; wherever I am, I go,' this was the little song of life and change and movement that came out of her curious heart and mind. 'Live on the run, like a bird, that's fun!' And by fun she meant life, and the soaring joy of life.

She applied her principle unconsciously to people, too. Few men had the bird in them except her father. Mother was a badger, half the time out of sight below the earth. She felt respect, but no genuine love, for mother.

'A whale or a badger, I really don't know which,' she said. 'That's Mother.'

'Joan, I cannot allow you to speak in that way of your parent and my wife.' The sentence was unreal. He chose it deliberately, as it seemed, from some book or other. What she had said was sparklingly true, only it could not be said. 'You were born out of mother, and so must think her holy.'

'I only meant that she is not birdy,' was the answer, 'and that she likes thick salt water, or sticky earth. I mean that I never see her on the surface much, and never for an instant above it. A fish is all right, but not a half-and-half thing.'

'She built your nest for you. She taught you how to fly. Remember that.' He lit his pipe to hide the laughter that would bubble up.

'But she never flew with me, father, as you do. Besides, you know, I like whales and badgers. I only say they're not birds.'

She paused, stared triumphantly at him a moment, and then with anxiety in her tone, she added: 'And you said that as if some one had taught it you, Daddy. Some one's put bird-lime near you, some book, I suspect.'

'Grammar's all right enough in its way,' he told her finally, meaning perhaps that there were correct and incorrect ways of saying a thing, and so the little matter was nicely settled up, and they flew on to other things as their way invariably was. But, after that, whenever mother was in the room, they thought of something under ground or under water that emerged for a brief moment to stare at them and wonder, heavens! how they lived. They wondered how, on earth, she lived. They were in different worlds.

For a long time now Joseph Wimble, 'travelling' in tabloid knowledge, had been absorbing what is called the Spirit of the Age. On the paper wrappers of his books, chiefly Knowledge Primers, were printed neat and striking epitomes of the contents. Written by expert minds, these epitomes were admirable brief statements. There was no room for argument. They merely gave the entire book in a few short sentences that hit the mind, and stayed in it. They left the impression that the problem was proved, though actually it was merely stated. Hundreds of those statements he had now read, until they flowed like a single sentence through his consciousness, each resume a word, as it were, in the phrase describing the knowledge, or at least the tendencies, of the day. Wimble was thus a concise phrase-book, who taught the grammar of the twentieth century.

For his Firm, alert and enterprising, had the gift of scenting a given tendency before it was understood by the mass, still 'in the air,' that is, yet while the mass still wanted to know about it; then of choosing the writer who could crystallise it in simple language that made the man in the street feel well informed and up to date. The What's-in-the-Air-To-day Publishing Co. was well named; it had the bird quality. These Picturesque Knowledge Primers sold like wildfire. They purveyed knowledge in tabloid form and advertised the hungry public into nourishment. The latest thing in politics, painting, flying, in feminism or call-of-the-wild, in music, scouting, cubism, futurism, feeding, dancing, clothing, ancient philosophy redressed, or modern pulpit pretending to be neo, everything that thrills the public to-day, from pageantry and Eurhythmics to higher thought and psychism, they touched with clever condensing accuracy of aim, and grew fat upon the proceeds. The stream of little books flowed forth, written by birds, distributed in flocks, scattered broadcast like seed in a wind, each picked up eagerly and discarded for the next, winged knowledge in sparrow doses. The Managing Director, Fox Martin (nee Max Levi), was a genius in his way, sure as a hawk, clairvoyant as a raven. His Bergson sold as successfully as his Exercises for the Bedroom, because he chose the writer. He hovered, swooped, struck, and the primer was caught and issued in its thousands. His advertising was consummate, for it convinced the ordinary man he ought to know that particular Thing-in-the-Air-To-day, just as he ought to wear a high collar with his evening clothes or a slit in his coat behind with flannels. He aimed at the men as the machine-made novel aims at the women.

Wimble, the traveller facile princeps, for this kind of goods, knew, therefore, everything that was 'in-the-air-to-day,' without knowing in the least why it was to be believed, or what the arguments were. And yet he knew that he was right. He knew things as a bird does, gathering them on every wind, and shaping his inner life swiftly, unburdened by reasoning calculation built on facts. Thus, useless in debate, his mind was packed with knowledge. He was a walking Index.

And the feeling in him that everything flowed and nothing was stationary was strong. He dealt in shooting ideas, not in dead, photographic detail. He flashed from one subject to another; flowed through all categories, ancient and modern; skimmed the cream off current tendencies, and swept above the knowledge of the day with a bird's-eye view, unburdened by fact or argument.

Of late, moreover, he had enjoyed these curious upside-down and inside-out experiences, because he had filled himself to the saturation point, and become, as it were, stationary. He could hold no more without a change. He stopped. He took a snapshot photograph of himself, realised that he existed as a separate, vital entity, and thenceforward watched himself expectantly to see what the change was going to be, for he knew he would not stay still. Hitherto he had been mechanical, whereas now he was an engine capable of self-direction, an engine stoked to the brim. When the air is at the saturation point, the tiniest additional percentage of moisture causes rain to fall. It's the final straw that makes the camel pause. So with Joseph Wimble. He was ready to discharge.

And it was this chance remark of his under-ground wife asking who the widow was that took the photograph, and made him say, 'I am.' All he had read was included in the affirmation. The epitomes had become part of his consciousness. Like the weary camel, like the moisture tired of balancing in the air, he wanted to sit down now and consider. His daughter's longing for the country was his too. And it was she who now brought out all this.

At dinner that night in a West End restaurant near Piccadilly Circus he broached the subject and listened patiently to his wife's objections.

'What's the good, even if we had the means, Joe? Burying ourselves like that.'

Joan hopped, as it were. She recognised her mother's instinctive dread that she would go under ground or under water and never come up again.

'None of the nice people, the county families, would call. There'd only be the vicar and the local doctor, or p'r'aps a gentleman-farmer or two. We know much better class in town, and there's always chances of getting to know better still. Besides, who'd there be for Joan? The girl wouldn't have a look-in, simply. And the winters are so sloppy in a country cottage. Think of the Sundays. And the chickens and pigs I really couldn't abide, and howling winds at night, and owls in the eaves, and rats in the attics. You see, we'd have no standing at all.'

'But just a week-end cottage, Mother,' Joan put in, 'just a place of flowers and orchards and a little stream to flit down to overnight, so to say, that now you'd like, wouldn't you?'

'Oh, that's different,' she said more brightly, 'only that's not what father means. He means a place to live in altogether. The week-end idea is right enough. That's what everybody does who can afford to, a bungalow on the Thames. But that means more money than we shall ever see, and even for that you want to keep a motor or a horse and dog-cart, or a little steam launch to get about in. Then the handy places are very expensive, and we couldn't go very far because of Tom. Tom could come down and bring his friends if it was near enough.'

'Grandfather might give us a little nest cheap,' suggested Joan. She didn't 'see' Tom in the cottage.

But mother turned up her nose as she sipped her glass of Asti Spumante that accompanied the west-end dinner by way of champagne. She didn't approve of Norfolk.

'There's no society,' she said. 'It's flat and chilly. Your grandfather only stays there because there's the business to keep going. If we ever did such a thing as to move to the country, it'd have to be the Surrey pinewoods or the Thames.'

She looked across the table questioningly at her husband. The music played ragtime. The waiters bustled. There was movement and excitement in the air about them. Joe looked quite distinguished in his evening dress, and she felt proud and distinguished herself. She only wished he were a publisher. Still, no one need feel ashamed of being interested in the book line. Literature was not a trade.

'Some place, yes, where the country's really alive,' he agreed. 'I don't want to vegetate any more than you do, dear, I can assure you.'

'Nor I, mother,' laughed Joan. 'I simply want to fly about all the time.'

'Joan,' was the reply, half reproachfully, 'you always talk as if we kept you in a cage at home. The more you fly the better we like it; I only say choose places worth flying to -'

Her husband interrupted abruptly.

'It was nothing but a little dream of my own, really,' he said lightly. 'A castle in the air, a flash of country in the brain.' He laughed and called the waiter.

'Black, white, or Turkish?' he asked his wife. 'And what liqueur, dear?'

'Turkish and Grand Marnier,' was the prompt reply, and she would have said 'fine champagne' only felt uncertain how fine should be pronounced. They sipped their coffee and talked of other things. It was no good, this speculative talk, it was too much in the air.

The key of mother's mind was always: Who was she? What'll they say? She lived underground, using the worn old narrow routes. Joan and her father made their own pathways in the trackless air. During the remainder of the evening they kept to the earth beside mother.

That night in the poky flat, after the girl had gone to bed, Mrs. Wimble observed to her husband:

'Do you know, Joe, I think a little change would do her a lot of good. She's getting restless here, and seems to take to nobody. Why not take her with you sometimes on your literary trips?'

This was her name for his journeys to provincial booksellers, or when sent to interview one of the Primer writers upon some practical detail.

'If we could afford it,' he replied.

'Father might help,' she said, showing that she had considered the matter already. 'It would be good for her, educational, I mean.'

Her husband agreed, and they fell asleep on that agreement.

A few days later a reply was received from Mrs. Wimble's father, the corn-chandler in Norfolk, enclosing a cheque for 20 pounds 'as a starter.' The parents were delighted. Joan preened her wings and began at once her short flying journeys about the country with her father. He avoided the Commercial Traveller Hotels and took her to little Inns, where they were very cosy together. They went from Norfolk to the edge of Wales. She acquired a bird's-eye knowledge of the map of Southern England. These trips gave her somehow the general 'feel' of the various counties, each with its different 'note,' in much the same way as the Primers gave her father his surface impression of England's mental condition. She noticed and remembered the living arteries which are rivers, he the streams of thought and theory which are tendencies. The two maps were shown and explained, and each was wonderfully alert in understanding the other's meaning. The girl drank in her father's knowledge, while he in his turn 'felt' the country as a dancing sheet beneath them, flowing, liquid, alive. A new language grew into existence between them, a kind of shorthand, almost a symbol language. They realised it first when talking of their journeys at the dinner-table, and Mrs. Wimble looked puzzled. Her face betrayed anxiety; she asked perplexed questions, looking up at them as a badger might look up at wheeling pigeons from the opening of its hole. Mentally she turned tail and dived out of sight below ground, where, with her feet on solid earth, her back and sides touching material that did not yield, she felt more at home, the darkness comforting and safe. Her husband and Joan flew too near the sun. It dazzled her. They could have talked for hours without her catching the drift, only they were far too fond of her to do so. They resented going underground with her, but they came down and settled on earth, folded their wings, used words instead of unintelligible chirrupings, and chatted with her through the opening of the hole.

One afternoon, then, in Chester, they received a telegram from her that, for a moment, stopped the flow of things, though immediately afterwards the rush went on with greater impetus than ever.

Father passed away peacefully   return at once   funeral to-morrow Swaffham.

And the family found itself with a solid little income of its own, free to fly and settle where it would.

CHAPTER VI

Nothing showed more vividly the peculiarity of Joan's unearthly airiness than the way in which the death affected her. It was the first time the great thing all talk about but none realise until they touch it, had come near her. It gave her a feeling of insecurity. She felt the solid earth, so called, unreal. Not that she had a feather of affection for her mother's father. She regarded him as a second-rate animal of prey, like a jackal, and always shrank when he was near. There was something 'sticky' in him; she classed him with her father's father, earthy, but not 'clean-earthy'; muddy rather. But that an earthy person could disappear in such a way made her feel shaky. If he couldn't stay on the earth, who could?

Outwardly, and according to the newspapers, he had died rather well, leaving money to hospitals and waif Societies; but, inwardly, he had died in deep disgrace, a bankrupt soul with a heavy overdraft at the bank. He had been a self-seeker of that notorious kind that achieves worldly success without much thought for others. Now that he was gone, mother declared he was a hero, father denounced him privately as ignoble, and their daughter divined secretly that he was a jackal.

His record, however, has nothing to do with this story, and is mentioned only because his departure affected the members of his family. Mother wept and pasted the obituary notices from the Norfolk papers in a book; father soothed her with 'earth to earth, my dear, you know,' and Joan remarked beneath her breath 'he belongs there, he never really left it.' And felt an entirely new sensation.

For death puzzled her. She realised it as a fact in her own life, she, too, would come to an end, stop, go out. Yet that life could come to an end astonished her; she simply didn't believe it. In her own queer way she looked into the odd occurrence. The corn-chandler's death had raised a dust; but it was an unjustifiable disappearance somehow; once the dust settled she would surely see how and why it was unjustifiable. He would still be on the earth. But the dust did not settle, the chandler did not come back. He was beneath the earth. The feeling of insecurity remained in her. Earth, evidently, was not her element.

She envisaged then suddenly a delightful thing, and possibly being a mere child still, in spite of her years, she actually believed it. It was wondrous enough anyhow to be worth believing. For it occurred to her that the body of earth went back merely to its own, earth to earth, sweetly, naturally, while Something that had used that bit of earth, borrowing it, was set free. It, that marvellous Something, likewise returned to its own element, air. 'The airy part, that's me, flies off, if it's there at all.' Only grandfather had made the mistake of identifying himself with his borrowed earth, so he was finished and done with. Mother had the same downward tendency. If she wasn't careful, she would be finished and done with too. It was a matter of choice. But how could they? How could any one? She and her father 'knew different', it was mother's phrase, and identified themselves with the airy part that was the reality.

She looked the thing in the face as well as she could, trying to hold it steady for a photograph. Death, to her mind, seemed to photograph the life it put an end to. The long series of acts and movements ceased. There came an abrupt full stop. Like a photograph this was somewhere, somehow, false. Wings folded for the last time; air failed for ever; there was a sudden drop to earth. Her grandfather, whom death had photographed, had gone, yet surely only gone, elsewhere; his record in the world of men and women was his attitude in the photograph; he was posing elsewhere now, but even he had not really stopped. Her little Song of Being did not mention anything of the sort. 'Flow, fly, stop! Wherever I am, I drop!' was merely wrong. A living thing could never end. It could neither drop nor stop. Some one had made a big mistake about death. She felt insecure.

And then she saw the matter differently, as though her mind made a sudden swerving turn into bright sunlight. And the sense of insecurity began to pass. This act of death revealed another meaning, connecting her with a vaster centre somehow, joining her up with a main central power. Death was returning to the main. She recovered the immense sense of unity she had momentarily lost. It made her realise that this tremendous centre, this main, was elsewhere than on the earth. Her conception of this unity deepened. To join the majority was more than a neat phrase. The photograph analogy came back of its own accord. Life here on the earth was indeed but a photograph, taken almost instantaneously though it seemed quite long, of a moment's pose. The shutter snapped, the sitter flashed elsewhere, flashed away to resume big interrupted activities, behind space, behind time, where no hurry was into a universal, mothering state she felt as air.

Man's life was a suburb of this state, a furnished house in that suburb, a Maida Vale tenancy, as it were; but there was this vast metropolis of air, the main, the centre, where the 'majority' lived, and whither all lines of flight converged. A thought of Everlasting Wings came to her with amazing comfort. And she realised that the insecurity she felt belonged to the suburb earth, rather than to herself. Others looked upon it as the one secure and solid permanency; for air was unsafe but earth did not change; air meant giddiness, absence of support, bewilderment, and terror of being lost, while earth stood for the reverse of all these dangers, permanent security. Her mother, for instance, simply dared not leave it for an instant. Whereas, it came to Joan suddenly now, that it was earth that crumbled, melted, got easily broken and dispersed, while air, though it moved, could never be destroyed. 'You can photograph earth,' she said, 'but no one has ever photographed the air.'

'A person just goes out, like that?' she asked her father, snapping her fingers. 'How can it be, exactly? Time ends for him: is that it?' Her face was distressed and puckered. She had no language to express the ugly thing that blocked her running, flowing mind. 'Once you're in among minutes, hours, years,' she went on, 'how can you ever get out of them? They don't stop.'

It seemed to her, apparently, that once a living thing exists it should not cease to exist unless Time, which bore it, ceased as well. And then another notion flashed upon her.

'Or perhaps they're just a trick,' she exclaimed, referring to days and minutes, 'and you've been alive somewhere else all the time too, and when you die you go back to that!'

Her father glanced up from the ordnance map he was studying and smiled with a sort of bewildered happy amusement on his face. Mother, however, turned with an uncomfortable sigh. 'That reminds me,' she stated inconsequently, 'I must go and sit in the Park.' She turned as a cow that prefers the rain upon its tail instead of in its eyes. 'I'll take a taxi, dear,' she added from the door. 'Do,' said her husband, suppressing with difficulty an intense desire to laugh out loud. 'Ask the porter in the hall. Or shall I call one for you?' 'The porter'll do,' she said. 'I'll go and get ready.' He said good-bye kindly, and she went.

'Time doesn't stop, of course,' he went on to Joan. 'You don't stop either, I suppose, if the whole truth were known.' He eyed her quizzically, for he delighted in her wild, nonsensical questioning. Behind it he divined that she knew something he didn't know, but only guessed. Or perhaps he had known it in his youth and since forgotten it. He remembered the ecstasy which had produced her.

'But why do we know a bit of the truth and not the whole? It's all one piece. It must be, father. What hides the rest, then?'

But he ignored the new questions. 'At death,' he said, 'you just go into another category perhaps. I suspect that's it. You continue, sure enough, but in another direction, as it were.'

Joan brushed the map aside and lit with a hop upon the table as though she fluttered down from above his head. Her hands rested on his shoulders, and her eyes stared hard into his own. They were very bright and twinkling. 'That's just throwing words at me,' she told him earnestly. 'That catty-thing, as you call it, isn't in our language and you know it. You nipped it out of a book.' She shook her finger at him solemnly. 'What I mean is', thrusting her keen face with its London pallor and shining eyes closer to him, 'how in the world can any one get out of Time, once they're in it?' She drew back as though to focus him better and command a true reply. 'Tell me that, please, father, will you?'

'That's a question, isn't it?' he said laughingly, yet not really trying to evade her. He wanted to hear her own answer, her own explanation. He knew quite well, had not the Primer on Expression said so? that the things they discussed in this way lay just beyond known words. Only by apparent nonsense-talk could they be brought within sight at all.

'It's a thing we ought to know,' Joan went on gravely. 'I do know it somewhere, only I haven't found it out quite.' Then, with another flash of her blue eyes, she stated: 'If a person goes from here, from now, I mean, they must go to somewhere else. I suppose they go back to the bigger thing. They go all over the place at once, perhaps.' And again she drew back a moment, staring at him as if judging height and distance before taking a breathless swoop down into a lower branch.

'Something like that, I imagine,' her father began. 'Time, you see, is only a point, a single point, the present. And if -'

But Joan was already following her own wild swoop, and hardly listening.

'That I can understand,' she said rapidly. 'You escape at death from a point where you've been stuck, like in a photograph. You go all over then.' Her mind tried to say a hundred things. 'I understand. That's easy. I'm an all-over person myself; I do several things at once, like a flock of birds or a great high wind. And when I do things like that they're always right, but if I wait and think about one of them, they go wrong and I'm in an awful muddle'

'Your intuition being stronger than your reason,' he put in with a gasp.

She did not notice the interruption; she had reached her tree; she saw a thousand things below her simultaneously, grouped, as it were, into one.

'But what I don't see plainly,' she returned to her original puzzle, 'is how a person, by dying, can get out of all this.' She flung her arms out wide to include the room. 'Out of all this air and stuff.'

'Space?'

'Yes, Space!' She darted upon the word with a twitter of satisfaction. 'I feel much more free among yards and miles, up and down, across and round and through, than I do just in minutes and days and years. Oh, I've got it,' she cried so suddenly that it startled him; 'Space is several things, and Time is only one. Space has throughth, you go through it in several directions at once. Time hasn't!'

He caught his breath and stared obliquely at her, for the fact was she was taking these ideas out of his own head. He had found them in his Primers, of course; now, she was taking them from his mind, sharing his knowledge by some strange, instinctive method of her own. In some such way, perhaps, birds shared and communicated ideas with one another. He felt dizzy; there was confusion in him as though he flew at fifty miles an hour through the air and was without support, seeing many things at once below. One of those moments was near when he stood upon his head. He was up a tree with the girl; he felt the wind; he, too, saw a thousand things at-once; he swayed.

'Space,' he mentioned, as soon as he had recovered breath, and drawing upon his inexhaustible reserve of Primers, 'has three dimensions, height, breadth, and length. But Time has only one, length. In Time you go forwards only, never back, or to the left or right. Time is a line. Don't pinch, it hurts!' he cried, for in her excitement she leaned forward and seized his coat-sleeve, taking up the flesh. 'So, possibly, at death,' he continued as soon as she released him, 'a person -'

'Goes off sideways,' she laughed, clapping her hands; 'disappears off sideways'

'In a new direction,' he suggested. 'That's what I said long ago, another category, where a body isn't necessary.'

'It's not a full stop, anyhow,' she cried; 'it's a flight.'

'Provided you've been already moving,' he said; 'some people don't move. They haven't started. And for them, I suppose, it's a biggish change, difficult, uncomfortable, painful too, possibly,' he added reflectively.

'They start for the first time, at death.' She ran to the window, but the same second was back again beside him.

'They get off the ground, off the map altogether. But they go into the air. They get alive,' and she picked the ordnance maps from the floor where her impetuous movements had tossed them. 'Death is just a change of direction then, really; that's all.' And the door slammed after her flying figure, though it seemed to her father that she might equally have gone by the window or the chimney, so swift and sudden was her way of vanishing. 'Bless me, Joan, how you do fly about, to be sure!' he heard his wife complaining in the passage. 'You bang about like a squirrel in a cage. Whatever will the neighbours say?'

She had taken all this time to clothe herself suitably for the Park. Mr. Wimble saw her to the lift.

'That's it,' he reflected a moment, before returning to search the map for a suitable country place to settle down in; 'that's it exactly. Mother says "Who was she?" and "What'll people say?" Joan says "Where, why, who am I?" Mother is past and Joan is future. That's it exactly. And I, well, what do I say?' He rose and looked at himself in the mirror with the artistic frame his wife had 'selected' at Liberty's Bazaar.

'I just say "I am,"' he concluded. 'So I'm present. That's it exactly.' He chuckled inwardly. 'Past, present, future, that's what we are! Yet somehow Joan's all three at once, a sort of universal point of view. Ah!' He paused. 'Ah! she's not future. She's now!' He caught dimly at the idea she tried to convey. To think of many subjects simultaneously was to escape time, avoiding sequence of events and minutes, obliterating, or, rather, seeing through, perspective which pretends that a tree ten yards away is nearer to one than the forest just beyond it. The centre, for her, was everywhere. To see things lengthwise only, in time or space, was a slow addition sum achieved laboriously by the mind, whereas, subconsciously, the bird's-eye view (as with the prodigy) perceived everything at once, making separate addition, or two and two make four, absurd. He was aware of a power in her, an attitude, a point of view, higher than this precious intellect which knows things lengthwise only, concentrating upon separate points, one at a time, consecutively. Joan knew everything at once. Her conception of perceiving things was all-embracing as air. She flew; wherever she was, she went. 'Throughth' was the word she coined to express it.

He felt very happy, there was a peculiar sense of joy and lightness in him, and yet he sighed. It was his mind that sighed. He was completely muddled. Yet another part of him, something he shared rather, was bright and clear and lucid. And, putting on his hat, he went after his wife and sat with her in the Park for half an hour, feeling the need of a little wholesome earth to counteract the dose of air Joan had administered to him.

They watched the people pass, the distinguished people as his wife called them, but actually the people who were dressed in the fashion merely, ordinary as sheep, shocked by the slightest evidence of originality, un-distinguished in their very essence. Mr. Wimble knew this, but Mrs. Wimble remained uninformed. The review of rich, commonplace types passed to and fro before their penny chairs, while they eyed them, Mrs. Wimble thinking, 'This is the great London world, the people whose names and dresses the newspapers refer to in Society columns. Oh dear!' Park Lane was the background; none of them dined till half-past eight; they kept numerous servants and were carelessly immoral, carelessly in debt, intimate with 'foreign diplomats,' reserved and unemotional, the aileet, as Mrs. Wimble called them. But, according to Mr. Wimble, they were animals, a herd of animals. They couldn't escape from the line of Time. They knew 'through' in Space, but not in Time. The bird-thing was not in them.

'Joan's coming on a bit,' ventured the father presently, trying to keep himself down upon the earth.

'If you call it coming on,' replied his wife, with a touch of acid superiority she caught momentarily from her overdressed surroundings. 'It's a pity, it seems to me. She's not English, Joan isn't, whatever else she is.'

'Oh, come now,' said Mr. Wimble cautiously, adding, a moment afterwards, 'perhaps.'

'It'll be the ruin of her, if we don't stop it in time,' came presently in what he recognised as her 'Park' voice. 'She don't get it from me, Joe.' Her words became inaudible a moment as she turned her head to follow a vision she imagined was at least a duchess, though her husband could have told her it had emerged, like themselves, from a suburban flat. 'I sometimes think the girl's got a soupsong of the East in her,' continued Mrs. Wimble, glancing with what she meant to be an aristocratic hint of wickedness and suspicion at her untidy husband.

'She may have,' he replied innocently, 'for all I know. Something very old and very new. It's not silly now, but it might become silly. She's too careless somehow for this world, and too wise at the same time. I can't make it out quite.' He looked up at the trees as the wind passed rustling among the dull green leaves. How blue the sky was! How sweet and fresh the taste of the air! There was room up there to move in. He saw a swallow wheeling. And the old yearning burned in him. He thought of the phrase 'bird-happy', happy as a singing-bird.

'It's a pity she's so peculiar. She'll make a mess of her life unless you're careful, dear.' Mrs. Wimble said it out of a full heart really, but she used the careless accent her surroundings prompted. She said it with an air. And, to her keen annoyance, the County Council man came up just then and asked for tickets, Mr. Wimble producing two plebeian coppers out of a dirty leather purse to settle the account. The pennies spoilt her dream. Money, but a lot of money, was what counted in life.

'Tom's doing exceptionally, I'm glad to say,' she resumed, by way of relieving an emotion that exasperated her. 'He'll make money. He'll be somebody, some day.'

'Tom's a good boy. He's safe and normal,' agreed her husband.

When the taxi had rushed them back to Maida Vale, and Mrs. Wimble had gone up in the lift, Mr. Wimble decided that he would like to go for a little walk before coming in. It was towards sunset as he ambled off. Joan, from the roof, watching the birds as they dashed racing through the air at play, caught sight of him below and waved her hand. But he did not see her; he did not look up; his eyes were on the ground. Yet he had a springy walk as if he might rise any moment. Joan watched him for some time, signalling as it were, making a series of slight movements and gestures that seemed a method of communication almost. Had he glanced up and seen her he must have noticed and understood what she was trying to say, as a bird on the lawn would understand what its companion, perched in the cedars overhead, was saying, distance no bar at all.

CHAPTER VII

And then, suddenly, he did look up. Feeling his attention drawn, he turned and raised his eyes to her. The rays of the setting sun fell on her dress of white and yellow. She looked like a bird showing its under-plumage. He waved his hand in return, instinctively making gestures similar to her own, and as he did so, a Flock of Ideas flew down upon him like a shower of leaves, nothing very distinct and sharp, but just loose, flying ideas that were in-the-air-to-day.

They seemed to result from the signalling; they interpreted something he could not frame in words. They fluttered about his mind, trying to get in and lodge. It was wireless communication, the kind used by animals, fish, moths, insects, above all, birds. He remembered the female Emperor-moth that, hidden in a closed box during the short breeding season, summoned the males across twenty miles of country until her antennae were cut off, when no male came near her. He felt as if Joan transmitted ideas to him, shaking them through the air from invisible antennae. He received the currents, but could not properly de-code them. He waved back to her again, then was lost to view round the corner.

'It's a queer thing,' ran through his mind, as though catching the drift of something she had flashed towards him, 'but Joan's got something no one else has got yet. It's coming into the world. Telepathy and wireless are signs, only she's got it naturally, she's born with it. She's in touch with everything and everybody everywhere, as though Time and Space don't trick her as they trick the rest. It's life, but a new kind of life. It's air life. That's what she means by saying she's an all-at-once and an all-over person. I understand it, but I haven't got it myself, and, as if to prove it, he ran into another pedestrian who cursed him, and, before he could recover himself, collided the next minute with a lamp-post.

The current that had been pouring through him was interrupted; it switched elsewhere.

'When more of us get like that,' it went on brokenly, 'when the whole world feels it', he snatched at an immense and brilliant certainty that was gone before he could switch it completely into his mind, 'it will be brotherhood! The world will feel together, one! It's beginning already. Only people can't quite manage it yet.'

And the strange lost mood of his youth poured through him, the point of view that made everybody seem one to him, when air and birds offered the dream of some inexpressible ideal. . . . He lost himself among the buttercup fields of spring . . . wandered through Algerian gardens where the missel-thrush sang in the moonlight and the radiant air was perfumed with a thousand scents . . . then pulled himself up just in time to avoid collision with a policeman who came heavily along the solid earth against him.

'Look where you're a-going,' growled the policeman.

'Go where you're looking,' he answered silently in his mind. 'That's the important thing, to look and to go!'

He steadied himself then. His mind scurried through the Primers, but found nothing that helped him much. Joan had asked him about Time and Space, and he had replied almost as though she had put the words into him first. Never before had he actually thought in such a way. Time and Space, as a Primer reminded him, were merely 'Modes under which physical phenomena are presented to our consciousness, under which our senses act and by which our thoughts are limited.' Both were illusory, figments of our finite minds; both could be subdivided or extended infinitely; both, therefore, were unrealities. They were false, as a picture is false that makes a pebble in the foreground as large as a cathedral in the background in order to convey so-called perspective.

And Joan, somehow or other, was aware of this, for she saw things all-at-once and all-over. He thought of her word 'throughth'; it wasn't bad. For she applied it to time as well as space. Time was more than a line to her, it had several directions, like space. He smiled and felt light and airy. Joan knew a landscape all at once, as though she had another sense almost. Every man believes he sees a landscape all at once, but in reality each spot is past by the time he sees it; it happened several seconds ago; he sees it as it was when the light left it to travel to his eye. Each spot has its separate now; there is no absolute Now. He had been wrong to tell her there was only the present; he saw it; she had flashed this into him somehow. To think the future is not there until it is reached was as false as to think his flat was not there until he stepped into it. He laughed happily, aware of a strange, light-hearted carelessness known in childhood first, then known again when he fell in love and so shared everything in the world. An immensely exalted point of view seemed almost within his reach from which he could know, see and be everything at once. Joan would know and understand what it meant; yet he had created Joan . . . and had forgotten . . . He thought of light.

By overtaking the rays of light thrown off from the battle of Waterloo he could see it happening now; if he moved forward at the same pace as the rays he could see Waterloo stationary; if he moved faster he could see the battle going backwards, of course. But Waterloo remained always there. Time and space were mere tricks. The unit of perception decided the childish dream of measurement. 'Ha, ha!' he chuckled. 'Real perception is for the inner self, then, omnipresent, omniscient, at-once and all-over.' To realise 'I am' was to identify oneself with all, and everywhere. 'Wherever I am, I go!'

'That's it,' he concluded abruptly, dropping upon a bench in a little Park he had reached, 'Joan doesn't think or reason. She just knows. She's an all-over and all-at-once person!' And he put the Primers, with their neat, clever explanations, out of his head forthwith.

'Cleverness,' he reflected, leaning back in the soft smothering dusk, 'is the hall-mark of To-day. It is worthless. It is the devil. It separates, shuts off, confines and crystallises what should flow and fly. Birds ain't clever. They just know. There's no cleverness in that Southern Tour, there's knowledge, all shared together.' The Primer writers, men who had made their names, were clever merely. By concentrating on a single thing they could describe it, but they didn't know it, because the whole was out of sight. They explained the bit of truth. Joan, ignorant of the photographic details they described and explained, yet knew the whole, somehow. But how? Wherever she was, she went!

He drew a long breath as if he had flown ten miles.

'She's something new perhaps,' he felt run through him, 'something new and brilliant flashing down into the old, tired world.' He lit his pipe with difficulty in the wind, fascinated by the marvel of the little flaming match. 'She's off the earth, a new type of consciousness altogether, sees old things in another way, from above and all at once. She's got the bird in her, 'Half-angel and half-bird,' he remembered with a sigh. Only that morning an essay on Rhythm in his newspaper, The Times, had mentioned: 'Angels have been called the Birds of God, and an angel, as we imagine him, is a being that can do all good things as easily as a bird flies. When we represent him with bodily wings we are thinking of the wings of his spirit, and of a soaring power of action and thought for which we have no analogy in this world except in the physical beauty of flight.' 'By Jove!' he cried aloud.

A flock of sparrows, startled by a cat, rose like a fountain of grey feathers past him, whirring through the air. There were fifty of them, but they moved like one.

'Got a whole flock in her!' he added.

He watched the fluttering mass of busy wings as they shot into a leafy plane tree overhead and vanished. A touch of awe stole over him. 'There's a whole flight of birds in her. She's a lot, yet one,' he went on under his breath, thinking that the fifty sparrows went out of sight like one person who turns a corner and is gone. How did they manage it? By what magical sympathy, as though one single consciousness actuated them all, did they swerve instantly together?

There was something uncanny about it. He felt a little creepy even. . . . The shadows were stealing over the deserted Park. A low wind shivered through the iron fence. A vast nameless power came close. . . . He got up slowly, heavily, and went out into the crowded street, glad a moment to feel himself surrounded by men and women, all following routine, thick, solid, reasoning folk, unable to fly. A swallow, flashing like visible wind across the paling sky of pink and gold, went past him. He looked up. He sighed. He wondered. Something marvellously sweet and lofty stirred in him. With intense yearning he thought of his little, strange, birdy daughter, Joan, again. His absorbing love for her spread softly to include the world. 'If she should teach them . . .!' came the bewildering idea, as though the swallow dropped it into him. 'Drag them out of their holes, show them air and wings, make them bird-happy . . . teach them that!'

A tremendous freedom, lofty and careless, beckoned to him, release, escape at full speed into the infinite air; all cages opened, all bars destroyed, doors wide and ceilings gone; that was what he felt.

But lack of words blocked the completion of the wild, big thought in him, for he had never felt quite like this since early youth, and had no means of describing the swift yet deep emotion that was in him. He could not express it, unless he sang. And he was afraid to sing. The County Council would misinterpret Joy. There was an attendant in the Park, a policeman in the road; he would be locked up merely.

CHAPTER VIII

He plunged into the stream of pedestrians and it struck him how thickly, heavily clothed they were; the street resembled a sluggish river of dark liquid; he struggled through it, immersed to his shoulders.

And the flock of curious, elusive thoughts, half-formed, fluttered above his mind just near enough to drop their shadows before they scattered and passed on. Much as a kitten pounces on the shadow of shifting foliage on a lawn his brain pursued and pounced upon them, bringing up the best words available, yet that did not suit because the necessary words do not exist. It was only the shadow of the ideas he captured.

'A new language is wanted,' he decided, 'a flying language, with a rapid air vocabulary, condensed, intense. Everything else is speeding up nowadays, but language lags behind. It's old-fashioned, slow. All these ideas I've got, for instance, ought to go into a word or two by rights. Joan put 'em into me just now from the roof by a couple of gestures, enough to fill a dozen Primers with words. Ah, that's it! What comes to me in a single thought, and in a second, takes thousands of words to get itself told in language. Words are too detailed and clever: they miss the whole. Aha! There's a new language floating into the world from the air, a new way, a bird-way, of communicating. We shall share as the birds do. We shall all understand each other by gesture, thought, feeling! Instant understanding means a new sympathy; that, again, means a divine carelessness, based on a common trust and faith.' And the immensely lofty point of view, as from a dizzy height in space, once more floated past him.

He steadied himself by pausing to look in at the shop windows. On a chemist's shelves he saw various things to stimulate, coax and feed people into keener life. The Invisible Sticking Plaster was there, too, to patch them up. Next door was a book-shop, where he remained glued to the window like a fly to treacle-paper. 'Success and how to attain It,' he read, 'in twelve lessons, one shilling'; 'Train your Will and earn more Money, fourpence halfpenny'; 'The Mysteries of Life, Here and Hereafter, all explained, sixpence net.' And second-hand copies of various books, marked 'All in this row tuppence only,' including several of the 'What's-in-the-Air-To-day' Primers.

Beyond was a window full of clothing, woollen garments guaranteed not to shrink; electric or magnetic belts, to store energy, 'special line, a bargain,' and various goods for keeping warmth in various parts of the body. All these shops, he reflected, sold things intended to increase or preserve life, artificial things, cheaply made, and sold to the public as dearly as possible, things intended to increase life and prevent its going. In other shops he saw mechanical means for stimulating, intensifying, driving life along. Life had come to this: All these artificial tricks were necessary to keep it going. Food, knowledge, clothes, speed that a bird possessed naturally in abundance. A robin's temperature in the snow was 110 degrees. Yet human beings required thousands of shops that sold the conditions for keeping alive, at a profit. He passed an undertaker's shop, to die was a costly artificial business too. There was too much earth in the whole affair. He remembered that no one ever saw a bird dead, when its death was a natural death. It slipped away and hid itself, ashamed of being caught dead!

A crowd collected round him, thinking he had discovered something exciting, and it jostled him until he elbowed his way out. He swerved dizzily amid the booming, thundering traffic, as he crossed the road and brought up against a toy-shop, where the sight of balls and butterfly nets, ships and trains and coloured masks restored his equilibrium. 'Real things are still to be had,' the fluttering shadows danced across his mind, 'And there are folk who like them!' he added in his own words, as two tousled-headed children came up and stood beside him, staring hungrily. He gave sixpence to each, told them to go in and buy something, and then continued his evening walk along the crowded pavement. 'Life is a great grand thing,' he realised, 'if we could all get together somehow. It's coming, I think. A change is coming, something light and airy penetrating all this, this sluggish mass, ' he broke off, again unable to express the idea that fluttered round him ' ah! it's good to be alive!' he went on, 'but to know it is better still. But you have no right to live unless you can be grateful to life, and create your own reason for existing. It means dancing, singing, flying!' He felt new life everywhere near him; a new supply of a lighter, more vivid kind was descending from the air. 'It's a new thing coming down into the world; it's beginning to burst through everywhere: a change, a change of direction'

He repeated this to himself as he moved slowly through the surging crowd. Joan, he remembered, had called death a change of direction only. But as he reached the word 'change,' it seemed to jump up at him and hang blazing with fire before his eyes. He had caught it flying; he held it fast and looked at it. The other shadows careered away, but this one stayed. He had caught the thing that cast it. The flock of shadows, he realised, were not cast by actual thoughts; they were the faint passage through his mind of mysterious premonitions that Joan's gestures had tossed carelessly towards him through the air. Coming ideas cast their shadow before. This one, at least, he had captured in a word, a figure of speech. He had pounced and caught it by the tail. It fluttered, but could not wholly get away.

Change was the keyword. A gigantic change was coming, but coming gently, stealing along almost like a thief in the night, emerging into view wherever a channel offered itself. Life was being geared up everywhere. Human activities, physical, mental, spiritual, too, were increasing speed. Humanity was being quickened. They were passing from earth to air.

Signs were plentiful, though mysterious. His mind roamed through the Epitomes of his Primers, skimming off the cream. Thinkers, artists, preachers, although they hardly realised it, were beginning to look up instead of down; from pulpit, press, and platform the little signs peeped out and flashed about the mass of expectant men and women. The entire world seemed standing on tip-toe, ready for a tentative flight at last. There was a universal expectation abroad that was almost anticipation.

But change involved dislocation here and there, and this dislocation was apparent in the general confusion that reigned in the affairs of the world. Stupendous hope was felt, though not yet realised and fulfilled. No one as yet could justify it. Pessimism and confidence, both strangely fundamental, were violently active. So long accustomed to terra firma, the world asked questions of its little coming wings, and the new element of air frightened even while it attracted, nervous, timid, wild, uneasy questions were asked on every side. Deprived of the old, comfortable ideas of Heaven and Hell, and suspicious of the newly hinted promise of survival, hearts trembled while they listened to so sweet whispers of escape into the air. The old shibboleths, distrusted, were slinking one by one into their holes. Science could, perhaps, go usefully no further; Reason, still proud upon her pinnacle, yet hesitated, unable to advance; Theology looked round her with dim, tired eyes. The whole starving earth paused upon a mighty change that should usher in a new and single thing, a new direction. Alone the few who knew, felt glad and confident, joy. But they felt it only, for as yet they could not tell it in language usefully.

They might live it, though!

'Live it, ah!' he exclaimed, and his thoughts came back again to his queer, birdy daughter. For Joan, he told himself, brimmed over with it. She had in her the lightness, speed, and shining of the new element; she was glad and confident, full of joy, bird-happy, aware of principles rather than of details. She sang. Of all creatures this spontaneous expression of joy in life was known to birds alone. No other creatures sang. The essential ecstasy that dwells in air, making its inhabitants soar, fly, sing, was liberated in her human heart.

True. . . . The weary world stood everywhere on tiptoe, craning its neck into the air for some new expected prophet who should take it by the wing.

It was a marvellous, delightful thought, and it sent his imagination whirring into space. The wings of his mind went shivering. He gave expression to it by a sudden gesture of his arms and head, making, it seemed, a spontaneous effort to rise and fly and, luckily, no one observed him making it. It was similar, however, to the movement Joan had made upon the roof as she stood outlined against the red and yellow sky; similar, also, to the flashing curve the swallow had shown him not long afterwards. It conveyed a thousand laborious sentences in a small spontaneous gesture that was rhythmical. Ah! there was a change of rhythm coming! And in rhythm lay a new means of instantaneous communication. Two persons in the same rhythm knew and understood each other completely, felt together. Then why not all?

The flock of shifting shadows fell more thickly down upon the floor of his receptive mind. He pounced upon them eagerly.

'Yes, it's an air-thing somehow,' he felt, watching the amazing pattern, 'a bird-thing coming. And she knows it. She's born with it.' He again remembered the buttercup meadows of Cambridge and the singing gardens of Algeria, the ecstasy, the light and heat of that exalted passion. 'Her mother had the germ of it, but in Joan it's blossomed out. People would call her primitive, backward, even a little crazy, 'hysterical' is the word they'd use to-day, I suppose, but in reality she's, er, awfully advanced. To be behind the race is the same as to be ahead of it, for life is circular and to run fast ahead is to overtake your tail. Signs of going back are equally signs of going forward. The same place is passed again and again until all it can teach has been caught from it; so the brain may be justifying scientifically To-day what was known instinctively to ancient times. The subconscious becomes the conscious.'

'No, no,' the shadows painted somewhere behind his thought, 'it's not circular, it's spiral. We come round to the same place again, only higher up, above, in the air. And with the bird's-eye view from above comes understanding.'

Joan, he remembered, had said a few days before, speaking of his button-hole: 'A flower is a stone put up several octaves.' That was flight in itself, all she said had flight in it. Her statement was true, literally, scientifically, spiritually, yet evolution was a word certainly unknown to her, and the spiral movement equally beyond her mental vocabulary.

The shadows danced and grouped themselves anew.

He reviewed strange signs that were-in-the-air-to-day, seeing them all as aspects of one single thing. They were not really disconnected; their apparent separation was caused by the various angles of survey, just as a floor seen from below became a ceiling. All that he was thinking now was, similarly, one big thing caught from various points of view. Some power swifter, surer than thought in him surveyed it all at once; the tiresome descriptions his mind laboured over took in the details separately, the shifting shadows; yet the pattern as a whole was in him, captured by some kind of instantaneous knowledge such as birds possess. Like Joan, he caught the bird's-eye view, in principle. Yet she refused to be blinded and smothered by the details, whereas they certainly muddled him. It was necessary to select the details one thought about evidently. He tried to stand outside himself and see the single something that included all the details, and in proportion as he did so he seemed to rise into the air.

He reviewed these details flashily, and, so doing, got a glimpse, an inkling, of the entirety whence they arose. All seemed to him significant evidence of one and the same vast thing; this new, queer, rushing supply of air-life flowing through everything everywhere, forcing a swift and rhythmical way in the most unlikely places, modifying human activities in all directions unaccountably. He saw a hundred of his Primer-Writers sitting in a studious group about it, each describing certain specific details, while the general outline of the whole escaped them individually. Each called his scrap by different names, little aware that all sat regarding the same one thing. It came up bubbling, dancing, pouring forth with rhythm, bringing lightness into solid details, unsettling the old-fashioned, and carrying many off their feet into the air. It was so brimming that it overflowed; to resist it brought confusion, insecurity, distress; to go with it was the only way to understand it, accepting the huge new rhythm. Yet it had so many guises, so many protean forms. Proteus was, indeed, a deathless truth, things changing into one another because they all are one.

He felt this new thing as synthesis, unity. The signs he reviewed combined in a single gesture that conveyed it. Earth, with its reason, logic, facts, could teach no more; Science was blocked from sheer accumulation of undigested detail; the new knowledge was not there; a new element was needed. And it was coming: Air.

Already there was a change even in sight itself, and artists saw things in a new direction. Mere foolishness to the majority, the cubists, futurists and the like presented objects to others, others quite as intelligent as the majority, quite as competent to judge, with an authentic fiat of truth and beauty. They conveyed an essentially new view of objects, warning the man in the street that the objective world is illusory and that concepts built upon the reports of the senses are radically deceptive. A city seen from an aeroplane resembled a cubist picture. This new sight seemed a bird's-eye view, again, though using, going back to, the primitive, naked, savage sight, yet a stage above it, higher, a tumultuous rhythm in it. The spiral again!

Side by side with it ran a strange new hearing too. The musicians, he recalled the names that showered through the Primer pages, called attention to this new hearing-from-another-angle. And, here again, it was a going back apparently. Debussy used the old, primitive tone scale, while Strauss and Scriabin, to say nothing of a hundred lesser ears, extended the rhythm of music to include the world of sounds as none have dared before. In literature, more swiftly assimilative and interpretative of the airy inrush, the signs were thickly bewildering. Only, for the majority, Pan being still misunderstood, the God of Air came more slowly to his own. But the signs were everywhere, like birds and buttercups in spring. The bird's-eye view, flashing marvellously, imperishably lovely, was on the way into the hearts of men, the fairy touch, the protean aspect, the light, electric rhythm running from the air upon the creaking ground, urging the mass upwards with singing, dancing, into a synthesis, a unity like a flock of birds.

The nonsense of unintelligible words and decapitated sentences tried to catch hold of what he felt, only failed to express it because it was too big for used-up, pedestrian language. He felt this coming change and swept along with it. He was aware of it all over.

It came, he realised, flushing the most sensitive, receptive channels first, the artists chiefly, and the apparent ugliness here and there was due to distortion and exaggeration, to that violence necessary to overcome the inertia of habit in a narrow groove, the tyranny of Mode. The accumulated momentum of habit flowing so long in one direction called for a prodigious rhythm to stop it first, then turn it back, into the new direction. Mode was the devil, der Geist der stets verneint, forbidding change, destroying innovators, worshipping that formal, dull routine which is ever anti-spiritual because it photographs a moment and fixes it to earth for always. . . . It was, of course, attacked, as all new movements are attacked, with contempt, with ridicule, with anger; but the attacks were negligible, and could not stay its gathering flow. The bright little minds of the day charged against it, stuck their clever shafts, and scuttled back again into the obscurity of their safe, accustomed groove. Mistaking stagnation for balance, they clung to the solid earth of years ago, but knew it not.

Of all this his mind did not frame, much less utter, a single word. But the pattern of its coming fell glowingly across his feelings. Life too long had been a single photograph; it seemed now a rushing cinematograph, revolving, advancing, mounting spirally into the air. He felt it thus. Something new was pushing up the map from underneath to meet the air; it was sprouting everywhere, going back to deep Pagan joy and wonder, yet with Reason added to it. Reason looked back breathless to

Instinct long despised and cried, 'Come! Help me out!' And into his mind leaped the symbolic image of a Centaur combining both these faculties. He added wings to it.

'Reason, oh, of course! Without reason who could know that at a certain station there must be a change of carriage?' The train and station once there, that method of roving once accepted, Reason was as necessary as a railway ticket. Only, well, he thought of the great Southern Tour and the perfect motion and perfect knowledge that led those tiny travellers to their distant destination and brought them home again to the identical hedge and bush and twig six months later. There was another way of communication. Birds knew it. The female Emperor-moth used it. Our wireless poles and instruments followed laboriously to achieve it. Yet the power itself lay in ourselves too, somewhere, waiting to be recognised without costly mechanism.

Yes, there surely was another way of travelling, of motion, coming, a bird-way, yet even swifter, surer still, because independent of the earthy body. The real, airy part of men and women were acquiring it already, their real selves, thought and consciousness, learning the new mighty rhythm by degrees. The transference of thought and consciousness was close upon them, from the air; wireless communication with all parts of space; the mysterious, unconscious wisdom of the bird, organised and directed consciously by men and women.

An immense thrill passed over him. He began to sing softly to himself, but so softly, luckily, that no one overheard him: 'Flow, fly, flow; Wherever I am, I go!' Joan knew it all unconsciously. She just sang it.

And bits of a bird-primer flew across his mind, casting the same delicate, protean shadows against the wall where thought stopped helplessly. The precocious intelligence of feathered life was still a mystery no primer-writer could explain. The curlew, he recalled, after wintering in New Zealand, paused to mate and nest in the South of England on his way to Northern Siberia, while awaiting the summons to complete its journey when the ice is gone. 'It is a fact, proved and attested beyond dispute, that the evening the curlew leaves the South of England is invariably the day on which the ice breaks in the north, at least two thousand miles distant.' How does the curlew know it?

He thought of the plover with five drums in his ear, able to hear the 'slow, sinuous movement of the worm in the soil, eight inches below the hard-crusted surface'; of the lapwing who imitates the sound of rain by drumming with his feet to bring the worms up; of the cuckoo matching her egg with those of the foster-mother selected for her baby, hundreds of variations; of the swallow, mating like the nightingale for life, and of a certain pair of swallows, in particular, who 'for fifteen consecutive years returned to the same spot, after wintering in Cape Colony, to build their nest, arriving invariably on the same day of the year, the 11th of April'; of the nightingales who winter separately, but return faithfully together to England in the spring, the female, perhaps, from India, the male from Persia.

A hundred marvels of air-life came back to him; all 'instinct', only 'mere instinct'! Birds, birds, birds! The wisdom of the birds! Their communications, their flocking together, their swift rhythmical movements, their singing language, their unity, their brotherhood!

From the air the new thing was rushing down upon the world, yes. Yet not alone the sensitive artist-temperament perceived it; it came overflowing into far less delicate channels as well, breaking up the old with difficulty, but producing first a tumult of disturbance that would later fall into harmonious rhythm too. There were everywhere new men, new women; behind the Woman Movement, for all its first excess, was a colossal, necessary, inevitable thing. Once rhythmical, the disorder and extravagance would become order, balance. The neuter woman was a passing moment in it, not to endure. The new woman was but another sign of the airy invasion which the painters and musicians, the writers and the preachers, felt. And the air-man, with new nerves, new courage, new outlook upon energy, even new bird-like face and strange lightning eyes, was another obvious, physical, yet only half-physical, expression. His audacious courage seemed somehow to focus the new consciousness preparing. The birds were coming everywhere. A new element, a new direction!

In advance of the invasion, making way for it, old solid obstacles were everywhere breaking down. He seemed to recognise a crumbling of religions, of religious forms. The rigid creeds and dogmas, made by man, and imprisoning him so long, were turning fluid before the stress of the new arrival, melting down like sand-castles when the tide comes in. They must hurry to adapt themselves, or else cease to exist. Formal, elaborate, dead-letter theology must go, to let in Religion. The churches seemed to have become unreal already, continuing, parrot-like, to teach traditional doctrines the people have long ago abandoned. He heard another Primer whisper in his ear. 'Every one is aware of the failure of the churches to touch modern life; to escape from their grooves; to cease to deal in conventional and monotonous iterations of old-fashioned formulae, instead of finding vital, human, developing expressions of the spiritual craving in man. They do not teach that the Kingdom of Heaven is on earth. They have isolated religion from practical life. Religion must evolve with the evolution of human culture' or disappear. Its teaching must take wings and rise to lead into the air, or remain stagnant on the ground in ruins, stony, motionless, dead, a photograph.

The 'wireless imagination' of the futurist was not so meaningless as it sounded. The exaggeration that preceded the new arrival would soon pass. Only, the first flight took the breath away a little, as when a man, from walking, breaks into a run to leap into an unknown element. Through the scientific world the quiver was running too. What's coming next? What in the world is going to happen? seemed the universal cry. The composite face of the world already assumed the eager lineaments of the great bird-visage. The air was coming.

The rhythm of life was everywhere being accelerated, and side by side with the mechanical expression in telephones and wireless communications, a quickening transformation of human sensibility was taking place as well. It was the running start for a leap into the air. Facilities for increasing the spontaneity of living existed at every street corner, but it was air that first produced them. Air made them possible. There was even approach towards the unification of the senses, one man hearing through his teeth and skull, another seeing through his temples. The localisation of sensibility was merging into a unified perception whereby people would presently know all-over and at-once. They would realise the eternal principle and ignore the obscuring details. Once they all felt together as the bird did, brotherhood, which is sharing all in natural sympathy, would be close. . . .

The shadow-patterns flashed and rustled on across his mind. In a couple of minutes all these wild ideas occurred to him. They were extraordinarily elusive, yet extraordinarily real. In an interval as brief as that between saying 'Quite well, thank you,' to some one who asks 'How are you?' this flock of suggestions swept over him and went their way. They never grew clear enough to be actual thoughts; they were just passing hints of what was in-the-air-to-day. All telescoped together in a rapid rush, marked him, vanished, yet left behind them something that was real. They came through his skin, he fancied, rather than through his brain. They came all over.

The pedestrians, meanwhile, shuffled past him heavily; he made his way with difficulty, the thick stream opening to let him through, then closing in again behind him. He felt closely in touch with them all, in more ways than one; but the majority were still groping on the ground, hunting for luxurious holes to shelter in. Only a few were looking up. He saw, here and there, an eager face turned skywards, tipped with the beauty of a flushing dawn. These, perhaps, felt it coming. But few as yet, one in a million, say, would dare to fly.

He watched them as he passed along, feeling them gathering him in. He saw the endless, seething crowd as a unit. He felt their strength, their beauty. He was aware of democracy, virile, proud, inevitable. He felt the hovering bird above it somewhere, immense, inspiring. The advancing tide was rising, undermining caste and class distinctions steadily, breaking down conventions, the feeblest sand-castles children ever built. He heard an awful thunder too. It revealed a storming majesty, shattering, cataclysmic, making most hearts afraid, the opening and stirring of multitudinous huge wings. Yet it was merely the new element coming, the great invasion with its irresistible rhythm. Democracy wore striped wings beneath its Sunday black, powerful, magnificent eagle-wings. Birds flying in their thousands, he recalled, convey sublimity. But yet he shuddered. The rising of such tremendous wings involved somewhere blood.

He saw, with his bird's-eye view, the general levelling up, or levelling down, in progress. No big outstanding figure led the world to-day. There were no giants anywhere. Much of a muchness ruled in art and business, as in statesmanship. No towering figures showed the way into the air. On the other hand there was degeneracy that could not be denied. He saw it, however, like the dirty flotsam seaweed pushed in front of a great high-tide. Degeneracy precedes new growth when that growth is of a different kind. Out of decaying wood springs a tree of fairer type, and from the ashes of a burnt hemlock forest emerge maple, birch and oak, while the flaming Fireweed lights the way with beauty. When a Canadian forest is destroyed by fire, the growth next spring is of a totally new kind, and no one has yet told whence came the seed of this new, different growth. After a prairie fire, similarly, new flowers spring up that were not there before. The subsoil possibly has concealed them; they are discovered by the fiery heat. The decay of old, true grandeur he saw everywhere, the democratic vulgarisation of beauty, the universal levelling up and levelling down, but he saw these as evidence of that crumbling of too in-bred forms which announced the new coming harvest from the air. It was but the decay of old foundations which have served their time.

'We shall build lighter,' he half sang, half whispered to himself, squeezing between a lamp-post and a workman who came rolling unsteadily out of a tavern door; 'birds'-nests, up among the swinging trees! We shall live more carelessly, and nearer to the stars! No cellars any more, no basements, but gardens on the roof! Winds, colours, sunshine, air! Oh!' as the man bumped into him and sent him off the pavement with 'Beg parding, sir!' 'No, I beg yours,' he replied, and came down to earth with a crash, remembering that supper was at seven-thirty and he must be turning homewards.

So he turned and retraced his steps, feeling somehow that he had come down from the mountain tops or from a skimming rush along high windy cliffs. The net result of all these strange half-thoughts was fairly simple. His imagination had been stirred by the sight of his daughter in the sunset making those suggestive gestures against the coloured sky. With her hands she had flung a shower of silver threads about him; along these, somehow, her own queer ideas flashed into him. A new point of view, a new attitude to life, something with the light, swift rhythm of a bird's flight was coming into the minds of men. Most of those who felt it were hardly conscious, perhaps, that they did so, because carried along with it. The old were frightened, change being difficult for them; but the young, the more sensitive ones among them at any rate, stretched out their arms and legs to meet the flowing, flying invasion. 'Flow, fly, flow; wherever I am, I go,' was in the air to-day. Joan knew. New hope, new light, new language, all aspects of joy and confidence, seemed dawning. Air and birds were symbols of it. It was rhythmical, swift, spontaneous. It sang. It was bird-happy and bird-wise. It was a new kind of consciousness, yet more than a mere expansion of present consciousness. It was a new direction altogether, while its object, purpose, aim was the oldest dream known to this old-tired world, brotherhood and unity. A bird brotherhood! The wisdom of the Flock!

'I declare,' he murmured, laughing quietly to himself, 'if any one could hear me, see inside my mind just now, they'd say I was -!'

And that reminded him of his wife. He remembered that he was thinking of moving into the country with his family before very long. He came back to a definite thought again. He pondered facts and ways and means. He was very practical really at heart, no mere dreamer by any means. He weighed the difficulties. Mother was one of them. Sad, sad, the bird had left her; she was a badger now. He felt uneasy, troubled in his mind. But he smiled. He was fond of her.

'How ever shall we manage?' he asked himself. 'There are so many incongruous things to reconcile. Gently, kindly, softly, airily is the way.'

Then, suddenly, a bird-thought came to help him. Ah, it was practically useful, this inspiration from the air. It was not merely nonsense, then!

'If I just hope and believe, and do my best, and don't think, too much, it will all come right. I must be spontaneous and instinctive, not overweighted by worrying and detailed reason. I must believe and trust. That's the way to get what's called good judgment. See it whole from the air!'

For the details that perplexed him were, after all, merely different aspects of one and the same thing, the several points of view of Mother, Joan, Tom, himself. Hold in the mind the details in solution, and the problem must solve itself. If he understood each one, that was necessary, while viewing the problem as a whole, the solution must come spontaneously of itself. The bird's-eye view would show the way, while he remained nominally leader, like the bird that heads the triangular wedge of wild geese across a hundred miles of sky. This flashed upon him like a song.

And as he realised this, his trouble vanished; joy took its place; with it came a sense of confidence, power, even wisdom. Though the matter was trivial enough, it was the triumph of instinct: Reason laid out the details, instinct pieced them together, then Intuition led. It was seeing all-over, knowing all-at-once. Already he had begun to live like a bird, and Joan, though he knew not how exactly, had taught him.

'Wherever I am, I go,' went darting through his head. He smiled, felt light and happy, and strangely wise. Perhaps he could help. Perhaps he was going to be a teacher even. A Teacher, he realised, must first of all find out the point of view of the person to be taught, and then discover a new point of view which will make the wrong or foolish attitude harmonise with reality. Everybody is right where he is, however wrong he may be. Only he must not stay there. The Teacher is a priest who supplies the new point of view. New teaching, however, was not necessary; the world was choked to the brim with teaching already. A new airy understanding of old teaching was the thing. . . .

He was now close to the iron gates of Sun Court Mansions, where he lived. In the diminutive, yet pretentious, plot of garden stood a tall, leafy tree. A gust of wind blew past him at that moment with a roaring sound that was like laughter, and he saw the tree shake and tremble. The countless branches tossed in a dozen directions, hopelessly in disorder, each branch, each twig obeying its own particular little rhythm. That they all belonged to a single, central object seemed incredible, so brave the show they made of being independent and apart.

Then, as he stood and watched, seventy thousand leaves turned all one way, showing their delicate under-skins. The great tree suddenly blew open. He saw the trunk to which leaves and branches all belonged. And at the wind's order the tree behaved as a single thing, even the most outlying portions answering to the one harmonious rhythm. At which moment, once again, a flock of birds rose from somewhere near with an effortless rush and swooped in among the leaves with one great gesture common to each one. They settled with the utmost ease. The myriad little busy details merged in one; they disappeared. But in settling thus, they made the solid green seem light as air, shiny, almost fluid.

And Wimble, taking the odd hint, felt too that his own difficulties had similarly turned fluid, melted, disappeared. The details merged into a whole; they were referred, at any rate, to some central authority that hid deep within him. A wind of inspiration, as it were, had blown him wide open too. Details that tossed in different directions, apparently hostile to one another, betrayed their common trunk. They showed their under-sides. He was aware of an essential unity to which all belonged.

Something in him shone. He had taught himself, at any rate. He went upstairs, confident and light-hearted, breathless a little too, as though he had enjoyed an exhilarating flight of leagues, instead of a two-mile trudge along the solid, crowded pavements of Maida Vale.

And later, when he went to bed, he fell asleep upon a gorgeous, airy conviction: 'The Golden Age lies in front of us, and not behind!' It was a birdy thought. He flew into dreamland with it in his wings.

CHAPTER IX

Mrs. Wimble felt the death in another manner. It disconnected her from life. It cut her off from a network of safe, accustomed grooves. Something solid she had clung to subsided under ground. A final link with childhood, youth, and beauty broke. Death has a way of making survivors older suddenly. Mrs. Wimble now admitted age to herself; wore unsightly and depressing black; felt sentimental about a big 'p' Past; and ruminated uneasily about other worlds. Black with her was an admission that an after-life was at best an open question. It was a lugubrious conventional act symbolical of selfish grief, a denial of true religious teaching which should have faith, and therefore joy, as its illuminating principle. She did not understand the question. She had no answer ready. She said, 'What?'

She referred to the 'lost' at intervals. It did not occur to her that what is lost is open to recovery. When she said 'lost' she really meant annihilated. For, though a Christian nominally, and a faithful church-goer, when she had clothes she considered fit for the Deity to see her in, her notions of a future state were mental conceptions merely that contained no real belief. She was not aware that she did not believe, but this was, of course, the fact. Her father, moreover, had long ago destroyed the reality of the two after-death places generally accepted, soon after he had taught her that they both existed. Not wittingly for his part, nor for her part, consciously. But since 'heavenly' was a term he used to describe large sales of corn, and 'Go to hell, you idiot' was a phrase he applied frequently to underlings in yard and office, his daughter had grown up with less respect for the actuality of these localities than she might otherwise have had.

And with regard to her love for him, it was not love at all, but a selfish dependence tempered with mild affection. He was now gone; she missed him. A prop had sunk, a tie with the distant nursery snapped, the sense of continuity with the fragrance of early days, of toys, of romance and Christmas presents was no longer there. Instead of looking backwards, still possible while a parent lives, she now looked forward into a muddled, shadowy future that brought depression and low spirits. It was a subterranean look. She went down under ground into her hole, yet backwards, still peering with pathetic eagerness into the sunshine of life that she must leave behind.

Therefore, for her father at any rate, she knew not love. For the one thing certain and positive about love is that those who feel it know, and to mention loss in the sense of annihilation is but childish ignorance. There is physical disappearance, separation, going elsewhere, but these are temporary, another direction, as Joan expressed it. Love shouts the fact, contemptuous of exact photographic proof. No mother worth her salt, at any rate, believes that death is final loss. She has known union; and Love brings, above all, the absolute consciousness of eternal union. 'Loss,' used of death, is a devil-word where love is, and as ignorant as 'loss of appetite' when food has become a portion of the eater. One's self is not separable from its-self. Love, having absorbed the essentials of what it loves, remains because it is; for ever indivisible; there. The beloved dead step nearer when their bodies drop aside. 'The dead know where they are, and what they're doing,' as Joan mentioned. 'It's not for us to worry in that way. And they're out of hours and minutes. They probably have no time to come back and tell us.'

To which Mother's whole attitude replied with an exasperated 'What? I don't think you know what you mean, child.'

Joan answered in a flash, her face clouding slightly, then breaking into a happy smile again: 'But, mother, what people think about a thing has nothing to do with the real meaning.'

'Eh?' said Mother.

'Their opinion doesn't matter.'

Mrs. Wimble bridled a little. She was not yet ready to be taught to fly. In this airy element she felt unsafe, bewildered, and therefore irritable.

'Then you'll find out later, Joan, that it does matter,' she replied emphatically with ruffled dignity. 'One can't play fast and loose with things like that, not in this world, my dear. One must be fixed to something, somewhere. Life isn't nonsense. And you'll remember later that I said so.'

Joan peeped at her sideways, as a robin might peep at a barking dog. A tender and earnest expression lit upon her sparkling little face.

'But life is a vision,' she said with a glow in her voice; 'it begins and goes on just like that,' and she clicked her fingers in the air. 'If you see it from above, from outside, like a swallow, you know it all at once like in a dream and vision, and it means everything there is to be meant. You put in the details afterwards.' She was perched upon the window-sill again, her long legs dangling. She began to sing her bird-song.

'There, there,' expostulated Mr. Wimble, who was listening, 'we're not birds yet, Joan, whatever we're going to be,' but the last seven words dropped unconsciously into the rhythm of her singing tune. He felt a wind blow from her into his heart. Mrs. Wimble, however, remained concealed behind her World. She was not actually reading anything, because her eyes moved too quickly from paragraph to paragraph. But she said nothing for some moments, and presently she folded the paper with great deliberation, laying it beside her on the table, and patting it emphatically.

'Visions are for those that like them,' she announced, moving towards the door and casting a sideways look of surprise and contempt at her husband whose silence seemed to favour Joan. 'To my way of thinking, they're unsettling. What time does Tom come in to-night?'

They discussed Tom for a few moments, and it was remembered that he had a latch-key and could let himself in, and that therefore they might go to bed without anxiety. But what Mrs. Wimble said upon this unnecessary topic meant really: 'You're both too much for me; my hopes are set on Tom.' She continued her perusal of the World in her room, retiring shortly afterwards to sleep heavily for nine full hours without a break.

CHAPTER X

Her father stood upside-down, mentally, of course, not physically. Certain of the Primer 'Epitomes' came in helter-skelter to support his daughter's nonsense. At the same time he was aware that he ought to chide her. And probably he would have done so but for the fact that before he knew it, the girl was asking to be forgiven. He had not seen her move; his mental sight was still following Mother. There was a flutter of something white across the air, and there Joan was, upon his knee.

And so he did not chide her. Nor did he rebuke her for singing under her breath what she called 'Mother's Song,' beginning:

O Disaster!   You're my Master!

'Your mother's tired to-night,' he observed. 'But all the same, you are a nasty little tease, you know.' Her arms felt like warm, smooth feathers as he stroked them. He seemed floating lightly in mid-air above the roof. And he remembered vaguely the fairy tales of his youth when Princesses turned suddenly into swans. Oh, how beautiful it was, this bird idea, this seeing and feeling things in the terms of birds. Those girls in Greece the gods changed into a nightingale and a swallow, what a delightful, exhilarating experience! Easy, and how true! 'The feathery change came o'er you,' he murmured from the Treasury of Song, then, interrupting his own mood of curious enjoyment, turned to Joan abruptly.

'Why did you talk like that?' he inquired.

'To make Mother move'

'To bed, you mean?' he asked, almost severely.

'Yes, no,' said Joan.

'Answer me properly, girl,' he observed.

'Of course not. Move nearer to you, and me, even to grandpa. We ought to be a flock somehow, I felt. But we looked so separate and apart, you two on chairs, reading, him out of sight, and me on the window-sill.'

'Eh?'

'We ought to be one thing more. The whole world ought to be. Not crowded, oh, there'd be heaps of room to move in, but all together somehow like birds. It's only bad birds that are apart, ravens, hawks, and birds of prey. All the others flock.' She darted from his knee and stood upon her toes a second before him, staring down into his eyes. 'It's coming, you know, Daddy. It's coming, anyhow!'

She said it brightly, eagerly, yet with a singular conviction in her tone. 'The whole world's flocking somehow, somewhere, for I feel it. We shall all be happy together once we get into the country.'

A shiver of beauty passed through him as he heard her. He remembered his walk up Maida Vale, and the rushing, shadowy presentiment in his mind that something new was on the way.

'Like a single big family, you mean? All after one high big thing together?' He asked it, greatly wondering at her. But her reply made him gasp. Where had she learned such things, unless from the air?

'Your language is so draughty, Daddy. I mean a bird-world. Birds aren't unselfish, they're just, together.'

He rubbed his forehead, saying nothing, while she fluttered down upon his knees again.

'Like my body,' she said. 'Don't you see?'

'Yes, no,' he laughed, using her method unconsciously.

'I can't lace my boot with one hand, but the other isn't unselfish when it comes to help. My head is no farther from me than my boot, is it?' And she sang softly her bird-song of movement and delight, until he felt the quality of her volatile, aerial mind flash down into his own and lighten it amazingly.

'My precious little daughter,' he cried, 'you are a bird, and you shall teach me all your flying secrets. But, tell me,' he whispered, 'how in the world did you find out all this?'

'Oh, I can't tell that,' she replied almost impatiently, 'for once I begin to think it all goes, and I feel like an animal in a hole. But I'll tell you soon, when the right moment comes, in the fields. I just go about and it all shoots into me.'

It was the true bird-quality, always singing, always on the alert, swift to notice and be glad.

'Yet I said it without thinking,' she went on, 'and the meaning came in afterwards at the end, all of its own accord. And that's really the way to live together. At least, it's coming'

'The next stage, the next move!'

'Flight!' she cried, half singing it.

'You live and talk,' he laughed, 'like a German sentence that carries all in the head and suddenly puts the verb down at the end.'

'Yes, yes,' he realised after she had gone to bed, while he sat there, pondering her fluid statements, 'there is this new thing coming into life, and it is in some sense indeed a bird-thing. It's a new outlook!'

He caught at her feathery meanings none the less. A great aerial movement had begun, an etherialisation, a spiritualisation of life. And in true spirituality there was nothing vague; its expression was terrifically definite, stupendously alive, swift, sure, and steady as a mighty bird. Spirit was a bird of fire. Joan left him in that dreary sitting-room with a feeling that life was glorious and that the entire population of the globe must presently take flight and wing its way to some less ponderous star, migration. Joan's language was absurd, yet she left winged ideas rushing like imperial eagles through his mind. Humanity was really one, but on earth alone it would never, never find it out. In the air it would. Its upward struggles were not mere figures of speech. Routine oppressed and deadened life, prisoning it within a network of rigid, fixed ideas, and behind barriers of concentrated effort which turned the fluid stagnant, hard. Routine was dulling, anti-spiritual. To live like a quicksand before you get fixed and sank, this was the way. To be ready for a fire that should burn up all you had. Life flows, flies, flows; it has rhythm and abandon; self, by means of boundaries and casting limits, resists this universal flow towards expansion characteristic of all Nature. A bird was poised. True! But it was ready to go in any direction instantly, for it was more various and less intense, by no means purposeless, and never bound. It was spontaneous, instantaneous, for ever on the run. That was living, that was 'fun.' People, like animals, were congested. But life was growing quicker, lighter, with rhythm, movement everywhere.

The shadow dance began again deliciously.

Yet to act intuitively seemed a dangerous plan for the majority at present, to live on impulse seemed mere recklessness. But it would come. Already people were tired of knowing exact and detailed reasons for all they did. Confusion would come first, of course, but out of that confusion, as out of the apparent trouble of a rising flock of birds, or the scattered muddle of leaves and branches in a wind-tossed tree, would follow magnificent concerted life. Democracy was growing wings. Soon it would sing for joy.

Yes, there was truth in it. Majestic powers were moving already past the visible curtain of fixed and rigid formulae. To obey an intuition the instant it came, was to find the opportunity at hand for carrying it out effectively. To wait and hesitate, consider, reflect and reason out, was to lose the chance. It was disobedience, and disobedience detached from power. Fate was controlled by an obedient and instantaneous mind, for it meant acting in harmony with these majestic powers. Understanding followed later, as with Joan's outlook; the verb came down at the end, explaining, justifying all that had preceded it. Good and evil were, after all, misnomers of the nursery. In rhythm or out of rhythm was common, aye, the commonest sense. Rhythm was simply ease, as separateness, due to want of rhythm, was dis-ease.

'Oh dear!' sighed Joseph Wimble, as he turned the light out and pattered down the corridor to bed. 'I feel carried off my feet. What a buoyant thing life is, to be sure! It gets big and light and happy when you least expect it! Evidently, there's a big universal thing underlying it all, that's what she means by air, and to lean upon that, subconsciously, I suppose, to act in rhythm with it' He broke off, colliding with a chest of drawers Mother would keep in the narrow passage.

Then, suddenly, as he switched the light on in his bedroom, he realised something very big and striking:

'Of course, I'm a cosmic, not merely a planetary, being . . .!'

CHAPTER XI

But what followed that night, while it may have caught him into the air, as he phrased it, and given him an airy point of view, took his breath away at the same time. He was not ready yet for so strange a revelation.

He did not sleep very soundly. Too many ideas were rustling in his brain. 'Rise out of rigid ideas,' a voice kept whispering. 'Hold ideas loosely in the mind. Cultivate agility of thought. Re-fresh, remake your thought. Destroy the hard walls that hide God from you. He is so close to you always. Shatter your idols and get free! Rise out of the network of fixed ideas! Watch life without sinking into your own personality. That is, share every point of view and think in every corner of your body. Grow alive all over. Don't think things out in your head; just see them! Embrace all possibilities! Get into the air! Melt down that absurdity, the scientific materialist, and show him LIFE!'

He heard these whispered sentences traversing the darkness like singing arrows whose whistling speed made a noise of words. Even in sleep he stood upon his head. But the arrows, of course, were feathered. They were feathers. Wings flashed and fluttered everywhere about him. He was in a cage. He must escape. He tried. Somehow, it seemed, he used his whole body instead of his brain alone. He was escaping. . . . Life, blown open by a wind, seemed to show its under-side where everything was one. . . .

By this time he was half awake. 'I must do something; I must act,' he dimly realised. He turned over in his bed, and the sound of arrowy, rushing air went farther into the distance as he did so.

'It's imagination,' sneered a tiny, wakeful point in his mediocre brain. Another part of him not brain was alight and shining.

'But you're no farther from Reality by letting your imagination loose,' sang a returning arrow, in his head. It came from something bigger than his mind. His mind, strutting and arrogant, seemed such an insignificant part of him, whereas the rest, where the arrows flashed and flew, seemed so enormous that he was conscious of the 'nightmare touch' of Size. Mind strove to justify itself, however, and Reason snatched at names and labels.

'But that's right,' a flying sentence laughed. 'You do not see a thing until you've named it. You only feel it. Once, however, it's described, it's seen!'

'Aha! That's Joan's fairy-tale method grotesquely cropping up in my dreams,' he realised, and so, of course, awoke properly.

And it was here that his breath got shorter and his heart beat irregularly.

The room was dark and silent, but he heard a murmuring as though Night were talking in her sleep. The dizziness of great heights was still about him, and remained a little even when he turned the lights on. It was four o'clock. The room wore a waiting, listening air, as though a moment before it had all been whirling, and his waking at this unlawful hour had disturbed it. Waking had rolled the darkness back, let in light, and taken a photograph. He felt mad and happy, madly happy. There was nonsense in him that belonged to careless joy. The curious notion came that he ought to introduce himself to the various objects, chairs, cupboards, book-shelf, writing-table, and apologise to them for having believed himself separate from them. He ought to explain. But the same second he realised this as wrong, for he himself had been moving, whirling, too. Everything had stopped, himself included, when he awoke. He had stepped aside to look at it. He had photographed it. Of course it stopped.

'I am,' he remembered, 'but wherever I am, I go!'

And then, before further Explanation could explain away the truth, he seized at another diving arrow and saw it whole, though it vanished the same instant:

'I am the whole room. I am my surroundings!'

Some new point of view had leaped into him, something almost daemonic that suggested limitless confidence in his power to overcome all obstacles, because they were part of his own being.

Objects, things, details, during that amazing second at least, no longer seemed separate, alone, apart from one another. They were not anywhere cut off. Seen thus, a chair was a cupboard, a table was a basin, he was the ceiling, bed, and carpet. Equally, a cat was a peacock, a mouse was an elephant.

He said these words to himself in an astonished whisper, and in doing so he understood something he didn't understand. The sentence waited for the verb, the meaning, and it suddenly came down pop at the end. Reason helped a little there, for he had named and described, and therefore seen what before he had only felt. Perhaps further understanding would follow. The verb would come. He would get up and try. He would do something, act, act out his mood. Action seemed suddenly a new kind of language, a three-dimensional language, an ever-moving language in which objects took on character and played parts for the sake of expression. A language of action! You are whatever you do. . . .!

And as this arrow shot its message past him it seemed that certain objects in the room were about to jump at him. They did not actually move, but they were just about to move, ready and alert. The instant he slept they would rise and fly together again. It was his point of view, his mind in him, that made them appear separate. Each object was clothed in its own story of information, as it were. Objects were telling him something. They were demonstrating an idea.

'I am not alone, although I'm only one,' he said aloud. 'In arithmetic one is not more lonely than seven.' But, again, he didn't understand quite why he said it, while yet he understood perfectly at the same time. 'I'm not quite myself at any rate,' he added, and it was true. Perhaps he was a trifle frightened, still hovering on the nightmare edge of sleep. For all this happened in a single instant when he turned the light up. With sight his breath came more easily at once, his heart beat steadily again.

Yet there was certainly a sense of rhythm in the room, though lessening rapidly. He must hurry. The cage was closing round him again. He heard the flying voices farther and farther in the distance, but still sweet with a rhythmical new music.

'Use the mood of the moment, but first understand why it is the mood of the moment!'

'Use the material you have at once! Don't wait for something different!'

'There is no need to wait; to wait shows incompetence!'

'Act instantly! Don't reason, calculate, think! Operate in a flash!'

He felt, that is, rather as a bird might feel. There was haste, yet no hurry, purpose yet leisure, delight without delay, spontaneity. So he got out of bed, put on dressing-gown and slippers, and went on tiptoe into the passage. Then, standing in the shaft of light from his room, the dark corridor in front of him, he realised that the entire flat, the furnished flat that Dizzy & Dizzy had let to him, was alive. The feathered arrows were not imagined, the voice was not a dream. Inanimate things stirred everywhere about him. He perceived their undersides and his own. Their apartness that so dislocated the upper, outer, surface-life was only apparent after all. Bars melted. He felt instantaneous. 'Wherever I am I go!' But objects shared the same illusion: wherever they were, they went! The sensations of a flock were in him. A new order of consciousness was close.

He paused and listened. No sound was audible. Mother's door was closed, but Joan's, he saw, just opposite, stood ajar. A draught blew coldly on him. He tapped gently and, receiving no reply, pushed the door wider and peeped through. The light from the corridor behind poured in. The room was empty, but the sheets, he saw, had not been lain in.

Recalling then her state of excitement when she went to bed, he searched the flat, peering cautiously even into Mother's room, but without result. The front door was bolted on the inner side. She had not left the building. He felt alarmed. Then a cold air stirred the hair of his head, and, looking up, he saw that the trap-door in the ceiling was open and that the ladder looked inviting. It 'jumped' at him, as he called it, that is it drew his attention as with meaning. So he snatched a rug from the shelf beneath the hat-rack, and, throwing it round his shoulders, clambered up on to the roof.

It was September and the sky was soft with haze, yet still empty and hungry for the swallows. Round balls of vapour pretending to be solid were being driven by an upper wind across the stars; but the stars were brilliant and shone through the edges of the vapour. And the night seemed in a glow. The wind did not come down, the roof was still; the mass of London lay like a smouldering furnace far below, bright patches alternating with deep continents of shadow. He heard the town booming in its sleep, a thick and heavy sound, yet resonant. And at first he saw only a confused forest of chimneys about him that rose somewhat ominously into the air, their crests invisible. Then, suddenly, one of them bent over in a curve, fell silently with marvellous grace upon the leaden covering; and, fluttering towards him softly as an owl, came some one who had been standing against it, Joan.

This happened in the first few seconds; but even before she came he was aware that the strange stirring of inanimate nature in the room below had transferred its magic up here. It was not discontinuous, that is, but everywhere. It had come down into the flat, as from the outside world, but the singular rhythm emanated first from here, above. Joan had to do with it.

It was exquisite, this soft feathery way she came to him across the London roof, swooping low as with the flight of an owl, an owl that flies so easily and buoyantly, it seems it never could drop. It was lovely. In some such way a spirit, a disembodied life, might be expected to move. He listened with eager intensity for the first word she would utter.

'Father,' she whispered, 'it's the Bird!'

He felt his entire life leap out on wings into open space. He had asked no questions. She stood in front of him. Her voice, with its curious lilt, seemed on the verge of singing. It came from her lips, but it sounded everywhere about him, as though delivered by the air itself, as though it dropped from the unravelling clouds, as though it fell singing from the paling stars. Night breathed it. And it frightened him, for a moment, out of himself. His ordinary mind seemed loose, uprooted, floating away as though compelling music swayed it into great happiness. His stream of easy breath increased. He touched that indefinable ecstasy which is extension of consciousness, caused by what men call crudely Beauty. Joy flooded him.

'The Bird!' He repeated the words below his breath. 'What do you mean?' Yet, even as he did so, something in him knew. 'A bird in her bosom' flashed across him from some printed page. The girl, he realised, had been communing with that type of life to which she was so mysteriously akin. Its approach had stirred inanimate nature into language. Meaning had invaded objects, striking rhythm, almost speech, from inert details. Joan had brought this new living thing, new point of view, into the very slates and furniture.

'The Bird!' he whispered again.

'Our Bird! Daddy.' And she opened her arms like soft white wings, the shawl fluttering from them in the starlight.

He ought to have said, 'Nonsense; go back to bed; you'll catch your death of cold!' Or to have asked 'What bird? I don't see any bird!', and laughed. Instead he merely echoed her strange remark. He agreed with her. Instinctively, again, he knew something that he didn't know.

'So it is!' he exclaimed in a whisper of excitement, taking a deeper breath and peering expectantly about him, as though some exhilarating power drew closer with the dawn. 'I do declare! The Bird, our Bird!'

He caught her hand in his. She was very warm. And, touching her, he was instantly aware of fuller knowledge, yet of less explanation. A sensation of keen delight rose in him, free, light, and airy, new vast possibilities in sight, almost within reach. He caught, for instance, at the meaning of this great rhythm everywhere, this impression that dead objects moved and conveyed a revelation that was so full of meaning it was almost language. Birds saw them thus, flashing above them, noting one swift, crowded series of objects one upon another. It was a runic script in the landscape that birds read and understood in long sentences of colour, shade, and surface, pages full of significant pictured outlines, turning rapidly over as they skimmed the earth. It was a new language, a movement-language. Birds read it out to one another as they flew. They acted it. Their language was one of movement and of action, three-dimensional; and, whether they flitted from one chimney to another, or travelled from Primrose Hill to the suns of Abyssinia, their lives acted out this significant, silent language.

High, sweet rapture caught him. Of course birds sang, where men only grunted and animals, still nearer to the ground, were inarticulate with unrhythmical noises.

All this flashed and vanished even while his eye lost its way in the canopy of smoky air immediately above him.

'Listen!' he heard in his ear, like the faint first opening whistle of some tiny songster. 'They're waking now all over England. You felt it in your sleep! That's what brought you up. It's the moment just before the dawn!'

A million, ten, twenty million birds were waking out of sleep. In field and wood, in copse and hedge and barn, in tall rushes by the lakes, in willows upon river banks, in glens and parks and gardens, on gaunt cliffs above the sea, and on lonely dim salt marshes, everywhere over England the birds were coming back to consciousness.

It was this vast collective consciousness that had awakened him. He had somehow or other taken on, through Joan, certain conditions of the great Bird-mind. It was marvellous, yet at the time seemed natural. He recalled the strange sentences: all descriptive of a bird's mentality, put into words, of course, by his own brain. The movement of objects was merely their new appearance, seen from above in rapid passage, all speaking, telling something, reporting to the rushing bird the conditions of the surface where they lay. And those at the point of lowest approach in the curve of flight appeared to 'jump.' The sense of rhythm, moreover, was the outstanding characteristic of feathered life, in song, in movement, in beat of wing, in swinging habits of the larger kind when migration regularly sets in and there is known that 'mighty breath which, in a powerful language, felt not heard, instructs the fowls of heaven.' He had responded somehow to the world of greater rhythms in which all airy life existed, and compared with which human existence seemed disjointed, disconnected, incomplete in rhythm.

'Air,' he remembered from one of the ridiculous Primers, 'is the highest perception we have, yet we need not be in the air to get this view. We have placed the Heaven within us up there, because it was, physically, our highest place to set it in.'

'Listen! and you'll feel it all over you,' Joan's voice reached him. 'I often come here in the dawn. I know things here.'

By 'listen' she meant apparently 'receive,' for no sound was audible except the hum of London town still sleeping heavily.

'So this is how you learn things! From the air?'

'I don't learn anything, in that sense,' she murmured quickly. 'It's in me. It just flies out, I see it.'

'Ah!' He caught a feather and understood.

'Especially when I go like this! Look, Daddy!' And she darted from his side and began on tiptoe a movement, half dance, half flight, between the crowding chimney-stacks. She vanished and reappeared. He heard no sound. The shadows clothed her, now close, now spread out, like wings whose motion just escaped the measuring eye. And the dance was revealing in someway he could not analyse. She seemed to bring the dawn up. The ugly roof turned garden, the chimneys shaded off into trees, as though her little dance flashed aspiration into rigid bricks. She interpreted the flight of darkness, the awakening of wings, the silent rush of dawn. No modern dancer, interpreting Chopin, Schumann, could have given a deeper, truer revelation. She uttered in her movements a language that she read, but a language for the majority at present undecipherable. Action and gesture interpreted the inarticulate.

She expressed, he was aware, the return to consciousness of the birds; but at the same time she expressed a new air-born consciousness that was stealing out of the skies upon a yet sleeping world.

'By doing it, I understand it,' she laughed softly, but no whit breathless, as she floated back to his side. 'But I can't tell it in words till long afterwards.'

The east grew lighter. The tips of the flying clouds turned red. A beauty, as of dawn in the mountains, crept slowly over the towered London world. It seemed the spires and soaring chimneys steadied down, as though precipitating a pattern from some intricate movement of the universe. Speech failed him for the moment. For the language of words is but an invention of civilisation, and he had just heard the runic speech that is universal and has no grammar but in natural signs of sky and earth. And then the words he vainly sought dropped into him suddenly from the air. Above him on a chimney crest a group of starlings fell to chattering gaily; hidden in the leaves of trees far below he heard the common sparrow chirrup; the earliest swallows, just awake, flashed overhead, telling the joy of morning in their curves of joy. In the distance trilled a rising lark.

The wonder and glory of that breaking dawn lay for him, indeed, beyond all telling; not that he had been insensible to loveliness in Nature hitherto, but that he saw new meaning in it now. In himself he saw it. The point of view was new. To Joan, however, it was merely familiar and natural. But more, he was aware that in him lay the germ, at least, of a new airy consciousness that included it all, and that he longed to share it with the still sleeping world below. A mighty spiritual emotion swept him.

'Mother would feel cold, and notice the blacks,' she laughed, but there was love and pity in her laughter.

For her it was all in the ordinary run and flow of habitual life. She was aware of no exalted state of emotion. She said it as normally as a swallow dares to take an insect from the heart of an amazing sunset. That sunset and that insect both belong to it. There was no need to be hysterical about either one or other.

CHAPTER XII

He woke in the morning and decided that his experience of the night had been a vivid dream-experience, although that was not to deny a deep reality to it. A sense of uplifting joy was in his heart that was the rhythm of some larger life. A new lightness pervaded his very flesh and bones; it sent him along the narrow passage to the bathroom, dancing, much to the astonishment of the cook who caught a glimpse of the phenomenon as she stirred the porridge; it made him sing while he sponged himself, waking Mrs. Wimble earlier than usual and stirring in her an unwelcome reminder that she was older, stouter than she had been. For the singing brought back to her a fugitive memory of a sunny Algerian garden, where life sang to a measure of blue and gold Romance, now vanished beyond recall. 'Joe's odd this morning,' she thought, turning over to sleep upon her other side.

But Joe, meanwhile, splashed in his bath and went on singing just because he couldn't help himself; his voice was meagre, yet it would come out. He dried himself, standing in a hot sunbeam on the oil-cloth that made him feel he caught the entire sun. Such a deluge of happiness, confidence, natural bliss seemed in him, seemed everywhere about him too. He could not understand it, but he felt it, and therefore it was real. In the rise and fall of some larger rhythm than he had ever known he swung above a world that could no longer cage him in. He saw the bars below him. Alarm, anxiety, worry, even death were but little obstacles that tried to trip him up and make him stumble, stop, and give up existence as too difficult to face. They lay below him now. He saw them from above. He was in the air. It made him laugh and sing to think that such tricks could ever have frightened or discouraged him. Actually they were but of use to stand on for a leap into the air, taking-off-things, spots to jump from into space.

'I can't explain it,' occurred to him, 'so it must be true.' It was a thing his daughter might have said. He shared her point of view, it seemed, completely now. They were in the air together.

And, though later and by degrees, the airy exhilaration left him, so that he came down to earth and settled, the descent was gradual and without a thud. Something of lightness and of wonder stayed. The memory of some loftier point of view guided him all day long amid the tangle of little difficulties that usually seemed mountainous. He rose lightly above all obstacles that opposed and hindered. He saw them from above, that is, he saw them in proportion. Stepping on each in turn, he flew easily over every one; they served their purpose as jumping-off spots for taking flight. It was the Bird's-eye point of view.

But each time he flew thus, he left his mind behind, using it as a cushion for landing later, easily, without a jarring bump. And thus, before the day was over, he realised somewhat this: that the instantaneous, spontaneous attitude Joan stole from the air and taught him meant simply that the subconscious became convincingly, superbly, conscious. The personality operated as a whole without friction or delay from separate portions that held back and hesitated. All these lesser, separate rhythms merged in one. It mobilised, as with a lightning instinct, the entire available forces of the being. He reacted to every stimulus as a whole, instead of in separate parts. Action and decision came in a single flash; to reason, judgment, the weighing of pros and cons, and so forth, he appealed afterwards. That is, intuitive knowledge became instantaneous action.

And, realising this, he also grasped what Joan meant by describing a room as 'happening all at once,' and found meaning also in her nonsense-dream of feeling for the one-ness of all life everywhere. The details of the room could be inserted later according to judgment and desire, and four-footed animals on the ground might also discover later the point of view of birds who, from a high altitude in the air, saw everything at once. Instantaneous action, immediate conduct, spontaneous behaviour enlisted the supporting drive of the entire universe behind them. Properly accepted, absolutely obeyed, such a way of living ensured inevitable success. It was irresistible; for since everything was one, each detail was the whole, and no whole could be disobedient or hostile to itself. And this was why he had danced along the passage-way and sung into his sponge.

Yet this attitude of mind, this point of view, was easily lost again; it was difficult to hold permanently; to practise, still more difficult. How to translate it into daily action was the problem. At breakfast this new language of action seemed mere phantasy. He certainly had enjoyed a dream of a three-dimensional language in which objects and things helped to interpret his own wishes; he remembered that distinctly; and surely it was not all imagination? Imagination, he felt sure, included prophecy as well as memory.

'It's time we found our country cottage,' he remarked, tasting his crisp Cambridge sausage and bacon. 'I must get to work at once.'

Mother glanced up over the morning newspaper she had crumpled till it looked like a bundle for lighting the fire. She had ignored the news and been deep in the advertisements. 'It's best to go to the agents,' she observed, folding the paper with the creases uneven and the pages mixed, then patting it into flatness. 'And if they're no good, we might insert an advertisement stating our exact requirements.' She mopped up a remnant of fried egg with a thick wedge of brown bread at the end of her fork. 'A nice neighbourhood's the chief thing, isn't it?'

Her husband straightened the paper so that the creases fitted evenly and the pages lay in sequence. It hurt him acutely to see it twisted; he felt something out of place inside himself, as though the feathers of a wing were tangled. 'It'll turn up,' he said airily, 'we shall come across it suddenly. I'll go and see some agents all the same, though,' he added. He had the feeling that the right place would hardly come through agents, but would just 'turn up.' Somehow he would be attracted to it: it would be there before his eyes; it would jump at him. He had already seen so many agents. Newspaper advertisements never mentioned it. This strange belief and faith was in him. 'I'll have a look,' he added, as his wife put the plates together, swept some crumbs carefully from the cloth, then tapped the marmalade spoon on the rim of the jar before she sucked it clean.

'There's no good just hoping and trusting to chance,' she said in a practical voice. 'Nothing comes that way.' She clicked her tongue, tasting the marmalade reflectively.

'On the contrary, everything comes that way.' To believe, he grasped, was to act with the Whole in which all that was required lay contained. 'Enquire within upon everything.' He laughed happily. But his wife had not followed his thought, nor heard him.

'That's turnip rind, not oranges,' she added. 'They sell you anything nowadays, and everything's adulterated' and laid the spoon aside.

'In the country we'll make our own,' her husband interrupted. 'Delicious stuff!'

'If we ever get there,' she replied, 'and if sugar ever goes down again, and we can get servants who'll condescend to stay. There's no good being too remote, remember, or we won't keep a single one. Servants won't stand being dull.' She sighed. Life to her spelt apprehension.

'Well, we've agreed on Sussex, haven't we?' he answered cheerfully, hunting for his lost new attitude again. 'A nice bit of wayward Sussex, where there are trees and fields and perhaps a snap of running water so that the birds'll come, ' he saw the cloud on Mother's face' Oh, but in a nice neighbourhood with decent neighbours,' he added, 'and a town not too far away, with a cinema and shops, and so on. Oh, it will come all right, Mother, don't you worry. We'll find it sure enough, probably this very day. I feel it coming; it's close already; I can almost see it at this moment.'

'It's there, waiting for us all the time. The very place,' said Joan suddenly, clapping her hands softly, and meeting her father's eye. 'Only we've got to want it enough and -'

'Tidy up your place, child,' said Mother sharply, 'and fold your serviette. It's time you were at your scales.' She sighed as Joan obeyed and left the room, and two minutes later, while Mother made notes on a squeaky slate for dinner, the sound of C major came to them through the wall, going rapidly up and down again with both hands. Only it was accompanied by a clear and happy voice that sang the notes, or rather sang a running melody to them that turned even the technical routine into music. The drudgery, though faithfully done, brought its fulfilment almost within reach. Like a bird, she leaped upon the promise and enjoyed it. Scales and music, toil and its results, prophecy and its accomplishment, even in this tiny detail, seemed present in her simultaneously. Carelessness and faithful plodding method went side by side. This came to her father as he lit his pipe and listened to the pure childish voice that unconsciously sang meaning, even beauty, into formal rigid outline.

'An all-at-once and all-over little creature,' he heard something whisper to him. 'Care-less and happy as a bird. The true air quality! That's the way, of course. I see it, a sort of bird's-eye view of beginning and end in one. The joy of fulfilment shining through the actual work. I'll find the cottage that way too!'

He puffed thick clouds of smoke between himself and his wife, who stood watching him, a touch of apprehension about her somewhere, impatience as well. She too was listening. He recalled the smile of the badger at the mouth of its hole. But, at any rate, it was a faithful, practical, and affectionate badger. Moreover, once, strange memory, it had known wings, it had been a bird! Wrong methods had brought it down to earth. It puzzled him dreadfully, yet rather sweetly. The bird, he fancied, must still lie hidden in her somewhere.

'Joan never can do one thing properly at a time, not even her scales,' she was saying. 'There she is, trying to sing before she's learnt her notes. I wish you'd speak to her about it. But, if you ask me, I think it's good money wasted, those music lessons.'

How right she was, he thought, from her point of view. At the same time, how entirely that point of view lacked vision. A badger criticised a bird for flying uselessly when there were eggs to be laid and worms to be pulled up and twigs for a nest to look at instead of rushing landscapes.

'I will, dear. I'll speak to her at once, before I go to see the agents. I'll bring back good news at dinner-time. Now good-bye, bless you.' He kissed her. She looked so helpless and pathetic that he kissed her again, adding 'Good-bye, old thing, don't worry. Take everything lightly like a bird and remember, Wherever we are, we go!'

'Good-bye, Joe dear. Do your best. You know our limit as to rent.' He noticed that for once she had not asked him to repeat.

He left the room and walked down the passage to admonish Joan, yet knowing that there was nothing he could honestly chide her for. She sang at her scales for the same reason he sang in his bath. In both of them, father and daughter, was the carelessness and joy of air, the certainty that, whatever they did on earth with effort, toil, and purpose, had in it, behind it and sustaining it, the glad sweet element of air. Air had no divisions, it was whole, a universal radiant element containing end and beginning, everything. To act with it instantaneously was to be confident that fulfilment lay already in the smallest germ of every action. 'The cottage lies there waiting for us now. Just look for it with faith and careless happiness. . . . The perfect music lies within these boring scales. Just sing to them. It brings accomplishment more swiftly near!'

But on opening the door and poking his head inside, he found that she had ceased singing and was diligently practising.

'That's right,' he said, smiling; 'it's rather dull, but stick to it. It'll please your mother, and before long you'll be able to play all my favourite pieces.'

She stopped, swung round on the stool and looked at him. Her little face in its wreath of shining hair was very earnest, the eyes big with wonder as though she had made a great discovery. He had seen a robin thus, perched on a window-sill, its head cocked sideways at a crumb of bread, poise, alertness, happiness in the attitude and gesture.

'Well,' he asked, 'what is it now? 'And pointing to the maze of black printed notes, she said: 'I only wanted to tell you something I've got hold of, There are only seven notes after all, only seven altogether.'

'That's all, yes.'

'All the music in the world comes out of that, just seven notes'

'Combinations of them, with a lot of half-notes too,' he explained.

'But half-notes only suggest. The real notes are the thing, just seven of them. Isn't it jolly? They'll never frighten me again. Now, listen a moment, Daddy, I'll play you what the wings sing when they rush along. You know, the sound in the air when birds fly past:

Flow, fly, flow,   Wherever I am, I go;   I live in the air   Without thought or care,   Flow, fly, flow. . . .

She played and sang till he felt every atom in his being moving rhythmically to the little doggerel. He took her in his arms and hugged her.

'Ah,' he cried, 'I put all this into you unconsciously, and now you're explaining it to me. That's fun indeed, isn't it?'

'And I've only used three notes for it, for the tune, I mean,' she exclaimed breathlessly as he released her. 'I've still got four more.'

He blew her a kiss from the door and went on the top of a 'bus to Dizzy & Dizzy, who gave him a list of orders to view some half-dozen desirable cottages and bungalows in Sussex that seemed reasonably within the price he could afford, but none of which, it so happened, was the thing he wanted.

And during the day, odd thoughts and feelings, born of that mystic dawn he had witnessed with the birds, came flitting round him. Being wordless, he could only translate them as best occurred to him. It was impossible to keep pace with many-sided life to-day unless a new method were discovered. To skim adequately among the numerous sources of information and instruction, wings were needed. With their speed and economy of energy the feathered mind could dive into all, absorb fresh knowledge instantly, and pass on swiftly to yet further sources. At present complete exhaustion followed the mere bodily and mental effort to keep abreast even with one line of thought and action. The bird's-eye view, involving bird's-eye action, alone could manage it. It was a case of flow, fly, flow, indeed. He was dimly aware of a new method coming softly, silently, from the air. Air meant the spiritual method. While the body, guided by surefooted, slow, laborious reason, attended to its necessary duties on the ground, the mind, the soul, the spirit would flow, fly, flow, with the new powers of the air. . . .

He played lovingly with the idea. He thought of birds as the aborigines of the air, the pioneers perhaps. They represent no climax of evolution. On the earth men appeared last, preceded by many stages of earlier development. Birds were, possibly, but the first, the earliest inhabitants of their delicious realm, still imperfect, but alive with a promise for mankind. They were not an ideal, they merely offered their best qualities to those below.

The Promise of the Air ran through him like a strain of glad spring music. Air, he knew, as Joan used the term, meant aether, the mother of all air. She dreamed of passages to dim old gleaming Hercules adrift in open space, to Cassiopeia, happily, mightily wandering, to the golden blossoms of the Nebulae's garden of shining gold. Across his mind the great flocks of stars were flying. . . .

'I'm not a "miserable sinner." It's a lie that "there is no health in me." Nor do I believe that another man can "forgive my sins," because I confess them to him, or that those who refuse to believe as I do, whatever it is I do believe! shall forfeit my special favours, least of all suffer the smallest prick of a pin on that account. . . .!'

If ever he had been affected by the dogmatic teaching of any person or group of persons, alive or dead, he broke finally with them in that moment.

CHAPTER XIII

Remembering his promise, though made only to himself, he proposed going to the cinema. Tom, who was present during the discussion that followed, wanted a Revue, but was overruled.

'You can't smoke,' he objected, but what he really meant was that he wanted to have his physical sensations stimulated by suggestive reminders that he was a breeding rabbit that had never left earth, earth which a single shower could turn into mud.

'That won't hurt you for one night, Tom,' observed Mother, aware vaguely of his difficulty.

They chose the best the advertisements supplied and went off after an early dinner. In a sort of bundle they started, Mother in her finery forgetting the performance was in the dark, Joan, smiling, neat and bright, her little ankles tripping, and Mr. Wimble important, holder of the purse-strings and full of anticipatory wonder. Tom, smoking cheap gold-tipped Turkish cigarettes, was superior and sulky. Like an untidy bundle the family made the journey towards Piccadilly Circus, a bundle with loose ends, patched corners, one end hardly belonging to the other, yet obviously coherent for all that, and with a spot of brilliant colour, Joan's bright, glancing eyes and eagerly pretty face.

Tom, having bought a halfpenny evening paper, read the sporting and financial news; his racing tips had proved false; his mood was ill-humoured; he eyed the girls on the pavement below, flicking his cigarette ash over the edge of the motor-bus from time to time.

'What's on?' enquired a chance acquaintance across the gangway, with an eye on pretty Joan. 'Music hall or high-brow legitimate?'

'Cinema,' returned Tom in a scratchy voice, 'with the family. I'm beat to the wide.'

'Who's put the wind up you this time?' enquired his friend.

'Family. They put it across me sometimes. Can't be helped.'

'Good egg!' was the reply, as the youth looked past him admiringly at Joan.

'Oh! my sister,' mentioned Tom, proudly, and with a flash of self-satisfaction; 'Joan, a friend of mine, Mr. Spindle,' adding under his breath something about Rolls Royce and Limousines, as though Mr. Spindle, who was actually merely an employee in some motor works, owned several expensive cars.

Joan, ignorant of the strange modern slang they used, nodded sweetly, then turned to watch the surging throng of energetic humanity on the pavement below. She was in the corner seat. Father and Mother sat below, inside. The sea of human beings rolled past like waves of water.

'Everybody going somewhere,' she said half to herself with a thrill of wonder. It struck her that, though hardly any one looked up, some must surely want to fly, and one or two, at least, must know they could. She wondered there were no collisions. All dodged and slid past and side-stepped so cleverly. The energy, skill, and subconscious calculation they used were considerable. In each brain was a distinct and separate purpose, a mental picture of the spot each busily made for, while yet all seemed governed by one common denial: that nothing off the earth was conceivable even. Like crowding ants, they stuck to the ground, shuffling laboriously along the world-worn routes. Their minds, she was persuaded, knew heavy ways, unaware that horizons are made to lift. She watched the herd in search for amusement after the drudgery of the day, engaged upon a common search. What they really sought, she felt, was air. Only they knew it not. In ignorance they toiled to find artificial excitement, pleasure.

She longed to lift them up and swing them loose into undivided space, let them know freedom, lightness, spontaneous carelessness. If they would only dance, it would be something.

'And all going to the same place,' she added aloud. She sighed.

'I hope to God they're not,' said Tom in his scratchy voice, thinking of the cinema.

'Eh?' remarked Mr. Spindle, with a thrust forward of his head.

The motor-bus lumbered into the Circus and drew up, leaning over to one side.

'So long,' said Tom to his friend, 'we push off here.'

Mr. Spindle offered his hand to Joan, who shook it, but looked past him, refusing the gleaming eye he offered her at the same time. They clambered down to their parents on the pavement, and joined the throng that swept heavily into the pretentious doorways of the cinema building. As they went in Joan glanced at her mother and realised that she loved her. She looked so worried and so helpless. It was pathetic how heavily she moved. Age! The age of the body, of course. But why should she be old? She was barely forty. She was out, seeking with a good expenditure of energy, for pleasure. It struck the girl suddenly that her mother's ignorance was singular. She knew so little. Somewhere about her, at the corners of her mouth, flickering in her opaque eyes, in the tilt of her ears, was still a vestige of youth and fun and joy. But Mother ignored it, crawling willingly with the herd. Yet the bird lurked in her surely. In spite of this heavy crawling, there were wings tucked away in her somewhere.

'Mother, we're out on a spree,' whispered Joan. 'Wherever we are, we go! Let me carry your bag?'

'Eh, Joan? What d'you say? Don't shove, my love. We shall get nowhere that way.' It was the Is-my-hat-on-straight tone of voice, self the centre. She yielded the tiresome bag gratefully.

'Everywhere, mother,' Joan whispered gaily. 'We'll get everywhere because we belong everywhere. Besides I'm not shoving.'

She glanced round at the other people, all pressing thickly towards the booking-office. All of them had troubles, joys, hopes, fears, and vague desires. All were out to enjoy themselves. Only their faces were so anxious, lined, and care-worn. They wore an enormous quantity of manufactured clothing, and each article of clothing represented similar joys, hopes, fears, and vague desires, complicated toil of those who had made and sold them.

She felt a curious longing, to collect them all together on the roof one morning so that they might dance and hear the birds sing at dawn. If only they could realise the bird-life and what it meant, care-less, happy, singing, dancing; deep purpose underneath it all, but that purpose not clogged with the stupefying detail of unimportant items. The trouble all had taken to clothe themselves suitably for this particular enjoyment was alone enough to kill any spontaneity. She smelt the fields, the keen, fresh air, the dew. She heard a lark rise whistling through the silver air. . . .

And she glanced back at her mother. Her mother was obviously adorned, with effort and difficulty. She looked as if she had walked through a Liberty curtain and parts of the curtain had stuck to her in patches. This complexity of cloth and silk and beads was wrong, funny at any rate. She sighed.

'It's all right,' said her father, catching the sigh behind him. 'We must take our turn, you know. But I'm out for the best seats, no matter what it costs.' It was like a breath of air to hear him say it.

'Extravagance,' put in Mother under her breath, overhearing. 'But it is an exception, isn't it?' Her mind fixed upon the difficult side of existence, the cost in labour and in pain.

'Eh?' said Wimble. He put his gaudy tie straight with a free half-finger.

'It isn't every night, I mean,' whispered Mother. 'It's an exception.' She looked challengingly at the listening crowd. It was very warm. The air smelt of people, clothes, and cheap scent. She was aware of scullery-maids, boot-polish, stable-boys, and wages. The ham in the larder, had they put the fly-cover over it? Oh dear, how sordid even enjoyment was!

'Move on, please,' boomed the deep voice of a policeman, and everybody moved on a step or half a step, casting looks of admiration, respect, and exasperation at the Great Bobby who represented rigidity, law, order, and that vague, distant power, the Government. To be spontaneous meant to be arrested, evidently.

'Wot've you got left?' asked Wimble mildly, facing at last the booking-clerk, then added quickly, 'Good. I'll take the three,' and put the money down. 'No, four, I mean; four, of course. How stupid of me! Thanks, thanks very much.' He had forgotten himself. Also, he had felt for a second that he couldn't afford the price, but yet somehow it didn't matter. It was stupid, it was extravagant, it was un-practical; no one in their senses could have approved his conduct. The clerk had explained briefly that no cheap seats were left; there was nothing under four shillings, and Wimble, without an instant's hesitation, had snapped up the expensive seats.

Joan witnessed it with a rush of joy. She saw her father slip several silver discs across the counter and take pink slips of paper in exchange. But it was not his extravagance, nor the prospect of greater comfort, that caused her joy; it was the unhesitating spontaneity. Daddy had not haggled; without hesitation he had taken the risk. He had flown. . . . In reality he could not afford it, yet only a stingy convention might have urged him to be careful. And he had not been care-full.

'Take no thought . . .' whispered a voice, was it Joan's? in his ear, as they pressed forward. And, as a consequence, he immediately bought several programmes where one would have been sufficient. Ah! They were in full flight. Their wings were spread. The earth lay mapped beneath them. In the silver, dewy dawn they flew. How keen the sweet, fresh air. . . .!

He looked at her. 'You don't earn the family income, my dear,' he observed drily, half-ashamed, half-proud. He fingered the pink tickets nervously, clumsily.

'But I will,' she replied. 'Besides, there's heaps for everybody really.'

'You're an unpractical absurdity,' he murmured, then gasped.

It was the child's reply that made him gasp:

'We're alive! So we deserve it.'

They swept the meadows and the pine copse in their flight. There was a crimson dawn. They smelt the sea, the wide salt marshes. Freedom of space was theirs.

Perhaps he didn't quite understand what she meant, yet it made him feel happy and careless. In a sense it made him feel spiritual. She had said something that was beyond the reach of language, of accurate language. But it was true, true as a turnip. It satisfied him as a mouthful of mashed potatoes, and was as easy to eat and swallow. What a simile! He laughed to himself.

'Be more accurate in your language,' he said slyly.

'And stick in grammar all your life!' she replied. They moved on. Tom looked superior and aloof. He did not belong to this ridiculous party.

'Hurry up, Daddy,' and Joan poked him in the ribs. 'Mother's waiting. You're thinking of your old Primers.' It was true. He had paused a moment. A sentence had flashed into his mind and made him stop, while Mother and Tom were waiting in the corridor beyond, something about the 'courage of a fly.'

A fly, the most fearless of attack of all creatures, an insect incapable of fear. He remembered that Athena gave Menelaus, in order that he might resist Hector, what? Not weapons or money or skill or strength. No. Athena gave him 'the courage of a fly.'

It struck him suddenly that the reckless courage of a fly, a fly that settles on the nose, the lips, the hand of a being enormously more powerful and terrible than itself, was unequalled among all living creatures. No lion or tiger dared the half, no man the quarter. But a fly, depending solely on its swift, unconquerable wings and power of darting flight, risked these amazing odds. He, in paying this high price for the tickets recklessly, had shown the courage of the fly: the sneers of Tom, the abuse of Mother, the scorn of cautious and careful convention. He had the money in his pocket, then why not spend it? His labour had deserved it; he had earned it; he was indeed 'alive.' Like an audacious fly he had settled on the nose of Fate. And all this Joan had snapped into a sentence:

'We deserve it. We're alive!'

'Is it all right, dear?' asked Mother anxiously. She was stuck with her elaborate flounces in a corner of the corridor. The programme-seller was at her elbow, pressingly.

'All right,' he replied, waving the programmes like a flag of victory, and led the way towards the seats. 'Everything's paid.' He bowed, dismissingly, to the girl. He walked on his toes.

They went in. Mother flounced down proudly, as though the cost, the risk, were hers. Anyhow, they had paid for their seats and had a right to them. Now they could see the show in comfort and with easy consciences. There was a vague feeling that too much had been expended, but it was discreetly ignored. Vanity forbade. Economy might follow. Let it follow. They could enjoy themselves for a few hours. They would enjoy themselves. Some one had paid good money and money well earned. Uneasiness was vulgar. Daddy's flying attitude influenced them all secretly, and the great human power of make-believe, so gingerly expended as a rule, asserted itself. They took the moment as birds take the air. They flew with him.

Settling themselves into their front-row seats, they fingered their programmes, and felt like Royalty.

Mother looked round her at the inferior human mass. 'We can see quite well,' she observed. 'You were lucky, Joe. You got good seats.' She was wholly unaware that she tried her wings.

'Not bad,' scratched Tom, equally unaware that he flew behind her, though parting from the sticky loamy soil with difficulty. Had his companion of the motor-bus been with him, he would doubtless have said 'Good egg!' instead.

'It's all right,' said Wimble. 'Like to see a programme? 'He passed over several, all he had. He felt uplifted, without knowing why. He felt reckless, extravagant, careless, happy. He had touched the element of air without knowing it. He had forgotten 'money,' toil, conventional rigid formality, the terror of the herd, everything that compressed life into a four-footed rut, like the rut trodden by cows and pigs and rabbits. He had, for a moment, left the earth. He had, however, no idea that he was hovering in mid-air. Having taken a risk with courage, the courage of the fly, he was not quite positive of his dizzy elevation. The strange, intuitive, natural certainty of Joan was not yet quite his. He caught his breath a little in this rarefied air, from this spiritual point of view, this bird's-eye aspect, he was by no means sure of himself.

The rush of the wonderful cinema then began, and he forgot himself.

They experienced the sense such a performance leaves behind of having been, as Mother put it, all over the place. Sitting in the dark the individual at first is conscious only of himself, neighbours ignored if not forgotten. The screen then flashes into light, and with the picture, consciousness flashes across the world. The lie of the stationary photograph is corrected, time is denied, partially at least, and space is unable to boast and swagger as it loves to do. The cinema frees and extends the consciousness, restores the past, and sets distance close beneath the eyes. Only the watching self remains, pregnant symbol! in the darkness.

It was one of the best performances in London; within an hour or two the audience danced from the dingy streets of the metropolis into the sunlight of India, Africa, and of islands among far southern seas. The kaleidoscope of other lands and other ways of thinking, acting, living carried them away with understanding sympathy. From savage wild life drinking at water-holes in the sun-drenched Tropics, they darted across half-charted oceans and watched the penguin and the polar bear amid arctic ice. Over mountains, down craters, flying above cities and peering deep under water, the various experiences of strange distant life came into their ken. They flew about the planet. The leaders of the world gazed at them, so close and real that their emotions were legible on their magnified features. They smiled or frowned, then flashed away, and yet still were there, living, thinking, willing this and that. Widely separated portions of the vast human family presented themselves vigorously, registered a tie of kinship, and were gone again about their business, now become in some sense the business of the audience too. Fighting, toiling, loving, hating, meeting death and adventure by sea and land, creating and destroying, differing much in colour, custom, clothing, and the rest, yet human as Wimble and his family were human, possessed with the same griefs, hopes, and joys, the same passion to live, the same fear of death, one great family.

Joan slipped her arm into that of her father; they nestled closely, very much in sympathy as the world rushed past their eyes upon the screen.

'We're flying,' she whispered, with a squeeze, as the penguins on the polar ice gave place to a scene of negroes sweating in the sun and munching sugarcane while they lazily picked the fluffy cotton. 'We're everywhere all-at-once, don't you see?' A moment later, as though to point her words, they looked down upon a mapped-out county from an aeroplane. The unimportance of earth was visible in the distance.

'You can't fly under water anyhow,' mumbled Wimble, as they left the air and flashed with a submarine upon sponges, coral, and inquisitive, perfectly poised fish. A black man was trying to knife a shark.

'I can see what they feel though,' was the whispered answer. 'Inside their watery minds, I mean.'

'Wherever I am I go,' he thought, but didn't say it, because by the time he had reflected how foolish it was to remain stuck only upon the minute point of his own tiny personal experience, they were climbing with a scientific Italian of eminence down a crater full of smoke and steam, and could almost hear the thunder of the explosions. But while they went down, everything else went up. Smoke, steam, masses of rock all trying to rise. 'Gravity is the devil,' he remembered; 'it keeps us from flying into the sun.'

The idea made him chuckle, and Joan pinched his arm, giggling too audibly in her excitement.

'Hush!' said Mother. They watched in silence then; a bird's-eye view of the planet was what they watched. With each picture they took part. Every corner of the globe, with its different activities, touched their hearts and minds with interest, busy, rushing life in various forms, and all going on simultaneously, at this very moment now. Life obviously was one. The strange unity was convincing. Nothing they saw was alien to themselves, for they took part in it. In each picture they 'wondered what it felt like.' They took for an instant, longer or shorter, the point of view of a new aspect of life, of something as yet they had not actually experienced. They longed, or dreaded, to stand within that huge cavern of blue lonely ice and hear the waves of the Polar Sea lick up the snow; to taste that sugary cane with animal-white teeth, and feel the fluffy cotton between thick, lumpy fingers; to swim under water and look up instead of down; to crawl fearfully a little nearer to the molten centre of the planet through smoke and fire and awful thundering explosions. They longed or dreaded. Mentally, that is, they experienced a new relationship in each separate case, a relationship that stretched a suburban consciousness beyond its normal ken.

'It's very tiring,' mentioned Mother, during a brief interval of glaring light, 'and hurts my eyes. And I can't see why they want to show us those half-naked natives. I'm glad I'm English. Disgusting people, I call them.'

'They'll improve it, you know,' observed Tom; 'the flickering, I mean. It's a great invention. Somebody made a bit of cash there all right.'

One couple, at any rate, in the four-shilling seats felt the tie and knew their consciousness extended to include them all. They were engaged with all these various folk and multifarious activities. Humanity was one. The cinema shouted it aloud. The sense of collective consciousness was stirred.

'Well,' gasped Mother, blinking her eyes in the sudden light at the end, 'that was a show, wasn't it?' She seemed tired rather than exhilarated.

'Not half,' declared Tom, feeling for his cigarettes. He kept the programmes, putting both into his pocket.

'I'm glad I'm English anyhow,' repeated Mother, stationary at the mouth of her hole in the ground; but whether she despised the Hottentots, the Eskimo, or the penguins, she did not specify. It was her final verdict merely. The statement said simply that she was satisfied to be her little self, balanced safely on a clod of earth, in a spot of the universe called England. Extension of consciousness gave her no joy at all. She felt unsafe.

They left the theatre slowly, their minds shrinking back with a touch of disappointment, almost of pain, within the prescribed limits of normal, practical life again. Wimble felt he had been flying, and had just come back; he settled with difficulty. In the brief space between the vestibule and the door his thoughts continued flying. There was excitement and anticipation in him. 'The next stage,' he said to himself, 'will be hearing. We shall hear the people talk. After that, not so very far away either, we shall see 'em now, and no interval of time at all. Machinery won't be used. Our minds will do the trick. We'll see everywhere with our thoughts!' He remembered his Telepathy Primer, giving individual instances, as authentic and well proven as any reasonable person could desire. He felt sure this vast, general development must follow, some faculty of air, swift and flashing as light, the bird's-eye view.

The murky street, with its damp and chilly air, struck him in the face as he stood with his family a moment, then walked down the steps. There was still a luminous glow in the western sky above the roofs. Mother took his arm to steady herself; Tom was behind, his eyes roving hungrily; Joan flitted just in front.

'Our 'bus is over there,' said Mother, pointing with a black-gloved hand.

'We'll take a taxi, my dear,' was his reply. He hailed one, bundled his astonished family inside, wished the driver 'Good-evening' with a smile, and slammed the door upon his own coat-tails.

'But you haven't told him the address,' said Mother.

'He ought to know,' exclaimed Wimble, 'but he's not a bird yet, so I'd better tell him.'

'It might be safer,' added his wife sarcastically, holding on to his coat-tails as he leaned out of the window to do so.

He watched the crowd as they whirled away; he felt happy, happy, happy. With the damp London air he felt as though a part of him still sweltered in the golden sunshine, diving under blue clear water where the sponges and the corals grew. Soft breezes touched his cheek one minute, the next he laid his hand on glittering ice. He heard the surf crashing upon a palm-clad reef. . . . These thronging people, policemen, costers, shop-folk, pale-faced workers, and over-dressed men and women of the big houses, all had some link with himself, that had been drawn closer; but so had the swarthy half-naked folk at the Antipodes who had just claimed his consciousness. They were all one really. Each nation seemed a mood. The sense of oneness leaped upon his heart and seized him.

'It all happened without our even moving,' as Joan had said on the way home. 'I suppose everything's in us then, really. We're everywhere.' And while Tom's superior 'Oh, cut it out' seemed more than usually ignorant and silly, Wimble's heart flamed within him. For it came to him, like a promise of wind-borne freedom, that there existed in his own being an immense and mighty underside that was only waiting to be organised into fuller, even into all-embracing, consciousness. Man, he felt sure again, was a cosmic, not only a planetary, being. He could know the stars. The real self was of air. . . .

CHAPTER XIV

'Look here, Father,' said Joan next day, 'why is it' then paused, unable apparently to express herself.

'Eh, child?' He gasped, thinking her question consisted of those three words alone, and wondering how in the world he was going to satisfy her.

'Why is it,' she went on the next moment, 'that wherever we are we want to be somewhere else, and whatever we know we want to know something else, more at any rate? And we never want it alone. We want to tell everything to some one else, I mean.'

Father almost preferred the first question, it left openings for vaguer answers. This definiteness increased his difficulty rather. He scratched his head and passed his fingers through his hair, which looked just then as if it would neither stay on nor down. He smoothed it deliberately, thinking as hard and quickly as he could. He knew what the girl meant, of course, more or less.

'The instinct to share what we like is, I suppose, a proof that we -' he was going to say.

Before he could utter the words, however, she answered for him: 'Because we ought to be everywhere at once and know everything at once, like in that cinema. Isn't that it?'

Mother, it so chanced, just then went past the open door along the corridor; she went steadily, not to say heavily; she was obviously in one place at a time, doing one thing at a time, a worthy, practical, useful human being, and what the world considers a valuable unit of humanity, yet surely, oh, surely, wrong and a wing-less entity clogged with earth and the limits that earth-ignorance involved. She was on her way to scold the servant, to order dinner, or to fetch socks to mend. Good. But it was the way she went about her job, the un-birdy way, that proved the badger in her. Air and the careless joy of air was nowhere in her, not even in her most helpful actions. 'One should take life as a bird takes the air,' he was thinking again. It had become a motto.

And a flood of shadowy thoughts swept down upon his mind. Joan, when he turned to find her, had already gone from the room. He was alone. The half-read newspaper lay upon his knee; Tom had long since gone to the office; the sun shone in across the sea of roofs and chimney-pots; he saw a white, soft, fluffy cloud bedded in the blue. A swift shot gloriously across the narrow strip of sky. And this flood of shadow thoughts poured in and out of his mind like a hundred thousand swifts.

They would have filled an entire Primer if written out and printed; but in his mind, together with their host of suggestive correlations, they flashed and vanished with the speed and ease of the swift, a bird that seemed only wings, without body, legs, or head, powerful, graceful flight personified. The laborious absurdity of words made him feel helpless and rather stupid. He felt lonely, too, exiled from a finer, easier state of being to which something in him properly and rightfully belonged. The wings of the spirit stirred and fluttered in him. He sighed. Joan's sentence vibrated in him like a song, for nothing so much as music sets free the bird in human beings, enabling the soul to soar beyond all possible categories of time and space, beyond all confinements and limitations, even beyond death.

It was his daughter's remark that led in this rushing shower of thoughts that followed: 'Why is it that, wherever we are, we want to be elsewhere?'

People as a whole were always afflicted with this desire to be somewhere else. It was true. In London he longed for windy lanes, but in the windy lanes he thought how nice it would be to see the shops and people in the streets; at a party he would think with longing of the cosy room at home, the book and chair beside the fire-corner with his pipe, yet in that corner with pipe and book he would suddenly lay them down and remember with envy the gaiety of company, the talk, the laughter, and the bright companionship he was missing. It was often, if not always, so: the desire to be elsewhere and otherwise seemed inherent in human beings; they were never content or satisfied with the place they were in at a given moment.

'It's the restlessness of the race,' he decided, 'for whom movement is so laborious, slow, and costly. If they moved as a bird moves, swiftly, instantly, and without trouble or cost, this restlessness would not be felt.'

Then he paused. 'But it's not merely that,' flashed through him, 'far, far more. It's the expression of a strange and deep belief: the belief that we ought to be, and should be, can be everywhere at once. This power lies in us somewhere, only as yet we haven't discovered how to use it. . . . But it's coming, and air and flight, wings and speed are already its beckoning symbols. We're being mysteriously quickened. We ought to be able to know everything, and to be everywhere, at once, in touch with all the universe, able to draw on all its powers. We have the right. This longing so to know and be, this uneasy yearning in us, what is it but an affirmation, a conviction that we can so be? Our wings go fluttering in our tiny cages. Wherever I am I go, and I am wherever my thought and desire are.'

He sat back and thought about it. It seemed to him a great discovery. He felt sure that somewhere in himself lay the power to be everywhere at once, one with everybody and everything. To be aware of everybody everywhere was the first step at any rate, and the cinema had dropped a hint that it was coming.

'Well, but the practical meaning of it, what? The use that people like Mother should make of it, what? Bodies will never actually fly. Certainly not, but thought flies already, and it only remains for consciousness to accompany it. Bodies, of course, are earth; yet they will, they must, grow lighter, more responsive, both as receiving and transmitting instruments, consciousness no longer focussed only where the body is. We shall be human cinemas,' he thought, 'going where we will, instantaneously and easily as a bird, seeing all and knowing all. Universal consciousness, of course, is a spiritual condition; it is an Air quality, space and time denied. The Kingdom of Air is within us. We shall experience air with its collective instantaneity. . . .'

He folded his newspaper and went down the narrow corridor to his little private den. 'Oh, that I had the wings of a dove,' occurred to him and made him smile. 'A cry of the soul, of course,' he realised, as he took his twenty limited steps between the rigid walls. He stubbed his toe against the desk, and sat down in his revolving chair.

The ideas set in motion by Joan's remark continued flowing, flying through him. He seized what he could catch.

'Our bodies, responding to a swifter, happier, more careless attitude of mind, will gradually grow lighter, more sensitive; become less dense and earthy; until at last we shall feel with everybody everywhere. No longer separate and cut off from others, divided as earth is divided, we shall win this immense increase of sympathy and be everywhere we want to be, every-at-once, as Joan put it. We shall move with our thought, air! We shall have instantaneity, air again! Our bodies may not fly, but our consciousness will fly to one another, as light flies across the universe unerringly from sun to sun, bodies of light. Like the birds in England, we shall know when the Siberian ice has broken. We shall be off!'

The thrill of some mighty wisdom came very near.

He became strangely aware, it was like the lifting of great wings within his soul, that this collective, airy consciousness was already gathering the world into a flock; and it was the cinema, explained by Joan's brief sentence, that flashed the amazing and uplifting thought upon him.

Whirling round and round in his revolving chair, reason tried to grapple with the rush of ideas. The contents of a hundred Primers rose higgledy-piggledy, to congest his mind and memory. But his soul, rising like a lark, outdistanced everything he had ever read. The one clear dazzling certainty was this: 'We shall no longer be cut off and separate from others.' A variant, surely, of loving, and therefore knowing, all neighbours as ourselves. A thousand years as one day! To be everywhere at once and to know everybody was, after all, but to slip the cables of the tiny, separate self, and experience the Whole. Hence the desire to be always elsewhere and otherwise. Hence, too, the innate yearning to share experiences of all kinds with others. 'Nirvana' dropped from a forgotten Primer into him, and for the first time pages of laborious explanation utterly ignored, he grasped its gracious meaning fully. 'To meet the Lord in the air and be for ever with him,' came another cliche. They poured and rained upon him in their naked meanings, undisguised by words.

'Ah! To live in the Whole was not, then, to lose individuality, but to extend and share it!' He spun round and round happily in his chair. 'Grand bird idea, and air ideal!' He saw in his heart the nations taking wing at last, leaving earth below them, free of space and free of time, sharing this new and undivided consciousness. It was spiritual, of course; yet not an inaccessible nor a different state; it was a state growing naturally and truly out of the physical. Spontaneous living and the bird's-eye point of view were the first faint signs of its approach. . . .

The chair stopped turning, while he filled and lit his pipe, watching the clouds of blue smoke float here and there in wreaths and eddies. Joan's eyes peered across it at him like a phantom's. . . . 'It's immense, but very simple,' he was thinking, 'her funny little song puts it all in a nutshell . . . and the way she tries to live . . .' when a heavy tread disturbed him and something came into the room.

'Joe dear!' said his wife as she entered, 'but you've got no air here!' She opened a window, while he at once sprang up and opened another. Her manner gave him the impression that she had come in with a definite purpose; she had something important she wished to say. He decided to let it come out naturally. He would wait.

'Not both,' she said, 'it makes a draught,' and closed her own.

'Bless you, my dear,' he exclaimed, 'you do look after me splendidly.' He gave her a sudden hug and kiss that startled her. Looking at him in a puzzled, wistful way, she smiled, and something of long-forgotten days slipped in magically between them for an instant. He saw a yellow scarf across the smoke; she saw perhaps, a breathless boy with a field of golden buttercups behind him. . . .

'You catch cold so easily,' she mumbled, then added quickly, 'the country will suit us all better, won't it?'

'Yes,' he answered, 'yet, once we're there, we shall want to be somewhere else, I suppose'

'Oh, I hope not, Joe,' with a Martha sigh. 'Whatever makes you think that?'

'We can be, anyhow; we must remember that.'

'Oh dear, Joe, you're very restless these days,' she exclaimed, and the way she said it made him realise her customary load of apprehension, her care-full, heavy way of taking life, seeing the difficulties first. Pessimism was a sure sign of waning life-forces. He felt pity and sympathy. And instantly an eddy of his recent whirlwind ideas swept down upon him and joy followed. He longed to communicate this joy to his wife, the joy she had known in her days of courtship long ago when the airy consciousness had touched her. And, as though to emphasise the contrast between their points of view, a wasp buzzed in through the open window just then, and Mother shrank.

In a flash he understood her very clearly. Her attitude to life was fear. Unable to leave the ground, she was always afraid of being caught. If she met a cow, it would toss her; a goat, it meant to butt her; a dog, a cat only waited an opportunity to bite or scratch, a wasp came in on purpose to sting her and not merely because it had lost its way. She invariably locked the door of her room and looked under the bed; she was nervous about lamps, they would blow up if she tried to put them out. Probably all these disasters would happen to her; her shrinking attitude of fear attracted the very thing she dreaded. People similarly would deceive her, since she expected, even demanded, it of them. In a word, the trouble she dreaded she attracted.

'Fly at anything you're afraid of,' he said suddenly. 'That paralyses it. It can't happen then. Or, better still, fly over it.' But she looked so bewildered, puzzled, even unhappy, that he got up and took her hand. 'Don't mind me, Mother dear,' he said soothingly; 'I've got an idea, that's all.' His heart brimmed full with comfort; her face said so plainly 'I don't understand, I feel out of it, I'm a little frightened! Only I can't express it quite.' 'It's immense but very simple,' he went on; 'Joan put it into me, I believe, first, and Joan was born out of us both, out of you and me, in those brilliant happy days when we were afraid of nothing. So it belongs to you, too, you see.' He paused, giving her an opportunity to state her mission.

'It's all a bit beyond me, I'm afraid,' said Mother patiently, an anxious expression in her eyes. But there was admiration as well. It occurred to her perhaps that she might have married a genius after all. She did not yet make her special and particular announcement, however. She would do so in her own way presently, no doubt.

'Mother,' he said abruptly, 'there's nothing in the universe beyond you.' He dropped her hand and stood erect, opening his short arms to the sky outside the window. The wasp buzzed out at that moment, and left him her undivided attention. His eyes were fixed upon the clouds where the swallows darted. 'Mother,' he went on, 'I'm illogical, unscientific, ignorant rather, and very confused in mind, in mind,' he emphasised 'but this immense idea beyond all books and learning has come to me, and I'm sure it's wisdom, though I call it Air.'

'Air,' she repeated slowly. 'Yes, dear.'

'Air, dear, yes, and that means living like the birds, more carelessly, more lightly, taking no thought for the morrow, not shirking work and duties and so on, but'

'But we know all that,' she interrupted. 'I mean, we've read it. It's this sort of having-faith business. It's all right for people with money.'

'The very people,' he corrected her, 'for whom it's most difficult.'

'Oh dear,' and she heaved another Martha sigh. There was a pause. 'Couldn't you put it in a book, Joe, write it?' she asked, pride in one eye and ambition in the other. He looked very much of a man, standing there so erect with his eyes fixed on space above her head. 'We could do with a bit extra, too.'

'And might help other people,' he added, 'eh?'

She said nothing to that. 'It might sell; you never know.'

He shook his head. He realised, once again, the pathos in her, and at the same time that she vampired him. It's the pathetic people that ever vampire and exhaust those who are more vital.

'I'm not literary,' he replied, 'not literary in that way. Only the few with air in them would catch my idea, and the others, the commonplace Press in particular which decides the sale of a book, would find a joke they could understand and call it air. And air is gas, you know.' He chuckled. 'Whereas what I mean is Air, instantaneous unifier of thought and action, the L.C.D. of a new order of existence, a new point of view born of collective sympathy, as with a flock of birds, community involving something akin to the strange bird-wisdom and bird-knowledge, ' he took a deep breath, 'the solvent of all philosophic and religious problems'

She caught a word and clutched it. 'Religious people,' she put it hurriedly, 'might buy it, a book like that.'

He came back from his flight with a thud, landing beside her. 'Their imagination is too sluggish, dear. As a rule, too, they have not intellect enough to detect the comic element in life. They can't laugh at themselves. They exclude joy and fun and play. They never really sing.'

'They do, yes,' said Mother, 'I mean they don't. That's quite true.'

She settled herself more comfortably in her chair. Evidently she appreciated his talking to her of his intimate thought; she felt herself taken into his confidence and liked it. It made it easier for her to say what she had come to say. Noticing her gesture his own sympathy and pity deepened. 'Ah, Mother dear,' he exclaimed, touched by a sudden pathos,' it's wonderful to be alive, isn't it? And to be able to think and feel ideas tearing about inside you? It's worth everything, just to be able to say "I am," and still more wonderful if you can add "I go." That's the secret. Live in the interest of the actual moment, but never imagine that it ties you there, eh? Life lies at your feet in a map; you can take what direction you please. Choice is your own, you can take or leave, as literally as when you stand above a jeweller's counter. One person chooses the bright stones, another the dark. It's all a matter of selection. On a picnic you may select the midge that stings you, the few drops of rain that fell, or the midges that did not sting you. . . . You can choose gloom or joy, I mean, just as you'

'Joe dear,' she interrupted, sitting forward in her chair, 'there's something I wanted to say to you, seriously.'

He took her hand again. He had noticed the growing pucker between her eyes and knew the difficulty she experienced in unburdening herself of something. He had chattered in this way to give her confidence and show his sympathy. But she had not followed, had not understood. She had remained safe in the mouth of her hole.

'Talking of religion, as you were just now,' she went on with an effort rather, 'I, I wanted to talk to you about it.' There was a hint, but a very tiny hint, of challenge in her voice.

'Of course, of course,' he said encouragingly, patting the hand he held.

There was a moment's silence, while their eyes met and he smiled into her troubled face. What she was about to say meant much to her, and she feared opposition. She took a deeper breath.

'I'm thinking of becoming High Church,' she announced.

'Admirable!' he exclaimed. 'I'm delighted!'

'What! You don't mind, dear?'

'It's just exactly what'll suit you,' he replied happily. 'Just what you need.'

'But very High Church, it means confession, you know,' she went on quickly, relieving herself of ideas evidently long pent up, 'and it must be very helpful, I think, knowing one's sins forgiven.'

'Helpful, and very pleasant,' he agreed, lowering his eyes from hers. The sudden sense of his own failure towards her pained him. She needed some one to lean on, to confide in, to unburden herself upon, and she turned to a paid official instead of to himself. She didn't know yet that she could confess to herself and so forgive herself, which meant understanding her sins and deciding not to repeat them. She needed some one who could do this for her. It was the stage she was at. 'Splendid,' he reflected, 'there were creeds for every stage. What a mercy!' And while she explained herself now without shyness, but with a confusion as great as his own, at his stage, he listened to her as vaguely as, doubtless, she had listened to him. He glanced down at his newspaper, not to read it exactly, but in the way a man who wants to think, to think subconsciously perhaps, takes up the object nearest to his hand and regards it attentively. His eye ran along the print, while his thought was: 'She wants something, some one to lean upon, of course, poor soul. I'm not sufficient, I don't give her sympathy enough. I'll do better in future. Her wings are on the flutter.'

' . . . Something to guide and help one a bit,' he heard her saying.

'The very thing, Mother, the very thing,' he put in. 'I'm so glad. It'll speed you up. Quickening, that's it, isn't it? Quickening of the spirit, and of the body too,' he added. 'You'll be flying with us next!'

And while she poured into his ears the confused but genuine story of her need, his own mind continued its own wordless thoughts. He saw the millions of history wading through the creeds, and, thank heaven, there were creeds enough to satisfy every type. For himself, a creed seemed to play the role of a porter in a mountain climb, carrying the weight from the climber's shoulders, but never guiding. Nevertheless, he blessed them all, and the Creed Primers in a long series with red covers and black lettering flashed across his memory. 'All true,' he realised, 'every blessed one of them. And no wonder each man swears by his own that it alone is true. For it is true; it's exactly what he needs.'

' . . . I was sure you wouldn't mind, Joe dear. I knew you'd understand,' came from Mother at last.

'And so you shall, dear. It'll help you along magnificently. We'll start the moment we get into the country, start it up, eh?'

'I have begun already,' she said, more sure of herself.

'Better still,' was his reply.

She got up, patted his shoulder awkwardly, kissed him, and stood a moment by his chair; a second later the door closed behind her. But hardly had her step died away along the corridor than the words his eye had rested upon absent-mindedly in the newspaper, rose and offered themselves. It was a coincidence, of course, but coincidences do occur. The sentence lay in the middle of a paragraph concerned with some new book or other, a book on Russia, he discovered, by glancing higher: '. . . She has a far-reaching vision, and her Church at least has for long been preoccupied with the idea of the union of humanity. . . . The idea of brotherhood and even universal brotherhood, permeates all classes of society . . .'; while opposite, and level with it in the adjoining column, oddly enough, was a notice of an article in some important Review or other with the title 'The New Religion.' The sentence quoted that caught his eye referred to the Church of England: 'A pitifully forlorn body, bankrupt in valour and policy, resource and prestige.' No one To-day with spiritual needs could, apparently, rely upon it; the new spirit regarded it as prehistoric. The people were far ahead of it already. . . .

He laid the paper down and wondered; the two statements capped his flying ideas so appositely.

'Yes, there's a new thing coming into life,' he exclaimed aloud. 'It's in the air, even in this vulgar halfpenny paper.' He relit his pipe and smoked a moment hard. 'Of course it's not generally realised yet,' he went on to himself between the puffs; 'but that's not odd after all: it's taken the world two thousand years to realise Christ, and only a few realised Him when He was there. When, how, will this new spirit touch us all . . .? What's got to happen first, I wonder?'

He sighed and a curious shiver ran down his spine. Nothing, he remembered, was born, nothing big and deep ever came to birth, without travail and upheaval. He was conscious of this strange shiver in his being. He almost shuddered. His pipe went out. Through the open window he looked down upon the crowded pavements, but the next instant looked up to where the swallows danced and twittered happily in the summer light and air.

The vision in Maida Vale came back to him when the masses, clothed in black, had seemed to rise and open a million mighty wings. He remembered the singular idea of blood that had accompanied it. And again a shudder touched him.

'Something's got to happen first,' he sighed, 'before all can take the air. Something's got to happen.' And then, as a burst of sunshine and cool wind entered the room together by the window, a sudden conviction swept him off his feet. The world blew open; the nations rose in a stupendous flock before his eyes; humanity as a unit spread its wings. 'something's going to happen,' he exclaimed, 'but out of it will grow the new birth of happy air!' There was both joy and shuddering in his heart, but the joy was uppermost.

He met his wife in the passage on his way out a little later. She button-holed him for a moment, a new confidence and lightness in her, it almost seemed. She was High Church now. It concerned their daughter. Joan, she mentioned, was not quite like other girls of her own age. She was growing very fast in mind as well as in body. She suggested a doctor for her. 'A London doctor, and before we go to the country. We might have her overhauled, you know. She seems to me light-headed sometimes.' Mother felt sure it would be wise. This time she was not anxious, did not worry as usual; she merely thought of the girl's welfare in the best way that occurred to her. From her new High Church pedestal she looked out upon the world with a temporary new confidence, at any rate.

'Admirable,' agreed her husband. 'I'll take her myself to-morrow.'

'Why not to-day, dear?' she asked, relieved that she need not go herself.

'We're off to look at cottages,' he told her. 'I'll take her to-morrow.' And the matter was settled thus.

CHAPTER XV

The visit to the doctor was a great success, and Wimble left two guineas on the marble mantelpiece without regret. Joan was growing rapidly in mind and body, and mind and body should develop evenly if possible, otherwise there must be unbalance somewhere. 'It's a nervous, restless age we live in,' observed the physician; 'the mind is apt to take in too much nourishment and shoot ahead much quicker than it did when we were young, Mr. Wimble, and unless the body is well cared for, the nervous system cannot possibly keep even pace with the mass of instruction it receives at every turn. The young it is wisest to consider as healthy animals that need play, food, and rest in right proportions. Personally, I prefer to see the mind develop a trifle late, rather than too early.' He advised, therefore, play, rest, and ample nourishment. 'Half an hour's rest in the afternoon, or better still, an hour,' he added, 'is an excellent thing.' He looked at Joan searchingly, with both severity and kindness, for he had that mixture of father and policeman which belongs to most successful doctors. Joan felt a little guilty. She had not read Erewhon, of course, yet was vaguely aware she had done something wrong. To be obliged to see a doctor touched the sense of shame in her. 'The country's just the thing for you,' the specialist mentioned, ignoring the two guineas that lay within the reach of his hand, 'the very place.' And Wimble felt relieved as he went out. It was like a visit to the police that had ended happily. Neither he nor Joan had been arrested, but they had been told they must not do it again. He had paid a fine.

'Mother'll be very pleased with that,' he remarked, while Joan, glancing up quickly, seemed glad it was over. 'It's the first time I've ever felt ill,' she said. 'The moment I saw him I felt I ought to be ill.'

'Suggestion,' he mumbled. 'Never mind. Mother'll feel better now that you've been. That's something.'

They walked happily down Seymour Street together. 'Don't skip, child. It looks funny in a town. Besides, you're too big to skip.' She took a slower pace to suit his slower little legs. But even so there were springs in her feet, and her movements seemed to push the solid earth away as though she wanted to rise. 'Flow, fly, flow,' she hummed, 'wherever I am, I go.'

'I shouldn't hum in the street, dear, if I were you,' he chided. People were staring, he noticed. 'It looks so odd. I mean it sounds unusual.'

She turned her bright, happy eyes upon him. 'Daddy, that's the doctor,' she warned him, 'you're saying "No" to everything.' She came close and took his arm, whispering at the same time, 'I believe you're sorry about the two guineas. You're trying to get your money's worth, as Tom calls it,' and the shaft was so true it made him laugh.

They turned down into the great thoroughfare of Oxford Street. It was brimmed with people, a river filled and running over. They crossed it somehow, he rather like a bewildered rabbit, a step forwards, a pause, a hesitating step backwards, a glance in both directions that saw nothing accurately, and then a flurried run; Joan catching his outstretched hand and pulling him against his will and better judgment, while his little coat-tails flapped in the wind. They landed on the curb, merged in the stream of pedestrians, bumped into some, collided with others, and were swept round the swirling corner of the Circus into the downhill torrent of Regent Street.

'Yet a bird,' he remembered, 'plunges headlong, at fifty miles an hour, into a forest of branches, swaying possibly in a wind, avoided the slightest collision, and with unerring and instant calculation selects a twig and lands on it, balancing with perfect security on feet so tiny they're not worth mentioning!' He felt clumsy and inferior. What co-ordination of sight and muscle! What confidence! What poise. . . . The throng of awkward, crawling, heavy-footed humans sprawled in all directions; he was one of them, one of the least steady too. And yet he was aware of something in himself that did not shake and wobble, something secure and balanced, something that went gliding with swift and certain safety. He noted the easy grace of Joan passing the shop windows like a nut-hatch along a twig, half dancing and half flitting on her toes. It was not a physical thing he felt. It was not that. It was a quality, a careless, exquisite balance in herself. It entered him too as he watched her. His soul rested securely amid the turmoil by means of it. It was poise.

His thoughts ran on. . . .

'Look, Daddy,' Joan interrupted him. 'Here's a funny sign. What does it mean? Let's go in.'

He drew up beside her, a trifle breathless. They were in a side street, the main stream of people pouring away at right angles now, bathed in the autumn sunshine.

'Look,' she repeated. 'Wings.' She pointed to a brass plate advertisement in a little hall-way. 'Isn't it funny?' He read the sign in neat black letters against the shining metal: 'Aquarian Society, Membership Free,' and wondered what it meant. Ruins and battered objects of the past occurred to him, for at first he connected the word with 'antiquarian.' Above them, black tipped with gold, were a pair of outspread wings, the badge of the Society apparently. In brackets was 'First Floor,' and a piece of paper pasted below bore a notice: 'Meeting Daily from 11.30 to 1. All welcome.'

'Let's go up, Daddy,' Joan said again. 'There's a meeting going on now, and it's free. What does it mean? Something about birds'

'Water birds, probably,' he said, still puzzling about the strange word; 'old water birds apparently,' he added, combining both possible derivations; 'perhaps a society to preserve old water birds and provide artificial paddles when their webbed feet wear out.'

They laughed at the idea, but their laughter hushed as a couple of ladies, beautifully dressed and with what is called refined, distinguished bearing, brushed past them and went upstairs, evidently going to the meeting. Though they were unknown to him, and it was obvious, in his black tail-coat and brown boots, that he was a commercial traveller of sorts, they bowed with a pleasant little smile of polite apology for pushing past. 'A duchess and her daughter at least! Old families certainly!' he thought; 'yet they treated us as equals!' It startled him, it was so un-English. He raised his hat and smiled. In their manner and the expression of face he caught something new, a kindness, a sympathy, a touch of light perhaps, something at any rate quick and alert and gentle that brought the word 'sympathy' intuitively across his mind. He held his hat in his hand a moment. 'They've got air in them,' flashed into him. 'I wonder if they're members.'

'Your head's in a draught, Daddy,' said Joan. He put his hat on. A scrap of conversation reached them from the stairs: 'I'd rather sit well at the back, I think,' said the younger of the two.

'We shall have to, probably,' was the reply; 'it's always full. And remember, just keep an open mind and listen. The quackery doesn't matter, nor the grammar. He was only a railway guard', then something inaudible as they turned the corner, 'his idea of a New Age is true somewhere, I'm positive. It was the speed of the train, you know, always rushing through space, that made him . . .' And the voices died away.

'Come, Joan, we'll go in too. What are you dawdling about for?' exclaimed Wimble on the spur of the moment. Something in that interrupted sentence caught him.

'You, Daddy,' she said, as she tripped after him up the stairs.

People were standing in the corridor and in the little hall; the room beyond, where a heavily-moustached man, with an eager, soap-polished face, cheerful expression, and bright earnest eyes, stood lecturing, was full. The two ladies who had preceded them were sitting on a window-sill. 'I'm afraid there are no seats left,' whispered a pleasant, earnest woman beside the door, 'but I've sent for some chairs. They'll be here presently. I hope you'll hear something out here.' Wimble thanked her with a nod and smile; he leaned against the wall with Joan and looked about him.

Some thirty people were crowded into the small inner room, three-quarters of their number women, what are called 'nice' women. They were well dressed; there was a rustle of silk, a faint atmosphere of perfume, and fur, and soft expensive garments; young and old, he saw, a good many of them in mourning. The men looked, generally speaking, like well-to-do business men; he noticed one clergyman; a few were shabbily dressed; one or two were workmen, mechanics possibly. There was an alert attention on most of the faces, and in the air a kind of eager expectancy, serious, watchful, yearning, and waiting to be satisfied; sympathetic, it seemed, on the whole, rather than critical. One or two listeners looked vexed and scowling, and a tall, thin-visaged man in the corner was almost angry. But as a whole he got the impression of people just listening patiently, people for the most part empty, hungry, wondering if what they heard might fill them. He was aware of minds on tiptoe. Here, evidently, he judged, was a group of enquiring folk following a new Movement. 'One of the Signs of what's in the air To-day,' he thought. 'Five years ago these people would have been in Church, convinced they were miserable sinners with no good in them. That mechanic-looking fellow would have been in Chapel. That portly man with the stolid face, wearing a black tail-coat, a low collar, a heavy gold watch-chain and a black and white striped tie surely took round the plate in Kensington.' The thin-faced angry man was merely a professional iconoclast.

He wondered. He thought a moment of the unimaginative English standing about the island in hordes, marvellously reliable, marvellously brave, with big, deep hearts, but childishly unobservant, conservative, conventional, not to be moved till the fire burns the soles of their feet, sturdy and unemotional, and constitutionally suspicious of all new things. He saw these hordes, strong in their great earth-qualities, ballast of the world, but at the same time world-rulers. . . . And then his thought flashed back with a snap to the scene before him. What was this group after? Why was it dissatisfied? Why had it turned from the ancient shibboleths? Something, of course, was up. He wondered. These people looked so earnest. This Aquarian Society, he knew, was one of a hundred, a thousand others. It might be rubbish, it might contain a true idea, it was sure to prove exaggerated. The people, however, were enquiring. He glanced at Joan, but her eyes were fixed intently upon the speaker's face, the face of a former railway guard whose familiarity with speed (certainly not on his own crawling line, thought Wimble!), with rushing transit from scene to scene through the air, had opened his mind to some new idea or other.

'I wonder if he sang "Wherever I am, I go!"' he whispered to Joan. 'He ought to, anyhow!' But Joan was too intent to hear him. He swallowed his smile and listened. The speaker's rough, uncultivated voice rang with sincerity. There was a glow about his face that only deep conviction brings. To Wimble, however, it all sounded at the moment as if he had fallen out of his Express Train and picked up his ideas as he picked up himself.

For at first he could not understand a single word, as though, coming out of the busy human street, he had plunged neck-deep into a stream of ideas that took his breath away. Having missed what had gone before, he could not catch the drift of what he heard. Then gradually, and by degrees, his listening mind fell into the rhythm of the minds about him; he slipped into the mood of the meeting; his intelligence merged with the collective intelligence of the others; he merged with the group-consciousness of the little crowd. The hostile interjections had no meaning for him, since those who made them, not being included in the group-consciousness, spoke an unintelligible language.

The speaker was very much in earnest evidently; he believed what he was saying, at the moment anyhow. Possibly this belief was permanent; possibly it was merely self-persuasion. Though obviously he expected hostile comment from time to time, when it came, usually from the iconoclast in the corner, he rarely replied to it. This method of ignoring criticism was not only easier than answering it, it induced an appearance of contemptuous superiority that increased his authority.

Wimble and his daughter had come in at a happy moment, for the long stretch of argument and explanation was just over, it seemed, and a summing up was about to begin.

'So where are we, then, with it all?' asked the lecturer. 'Where 'ave we got to? Where do we stand?'

He paused, and into the pause fell the angry voice of the thin-faced man: 'Exactly where we started. You haven't stated one single fact as yet.'

The speaker looked straight in front of him without a word, and the audience, almost to an individual, ignored the criticism. They supported the lecturer loyally, to the point at least of not even turning their heads away. They stared patiently and waited.

'Where 'ave we got to,' repeated the man on the platform, 'that's wot we want to know, isn't it? After all we've listened to this morning, 'ow do we stand about it?'

'That's it exactly,' from the interrupter in a contemptuous but intense tone of voice. He seemed annoyed that no one was intelligent enough to support him. At a Society of Rationalist Control across the road he would have been at home. He, too, was a seeker, and a very earnest one, only he had tumbled into the wrong group. Across the road he might have been constructive; here he was destructive merely.

'Well, on the physical plane,' resumed the speaker, 'on wot I might call the scientific and materialistic plane, as I've tried to show you, the 'ole trend of modern civilisation is towards speed and universality. That's clear, at least I 'ope I've made it so. Air, and wot air represents, shows itself in the physical plane like that. Distant countries are getting all linked up everywhere, by wireless, by motor, by aviation, by cinematograph, and the like. A kind of telepathy all over the world is, ' he hesitated an instant, 'engendered.'

'Go on,' from the critic, 'any word will do as well.'

'That's the scientific side of the business, as it were,' he went on, 'the practical, everyday aspect we can all understand. It's the universality of the new element, air, as it affects the practical mind, so to speak; the technical understanding and mastery or space, wot I called aether a little while ago, as you'll remember, or, as the Aquarian Society prefers to call it, as being simpler and shorter, air.'

'Well,' he added, 'we now want to see 'ow we stand with regard to the 'igher side of life, the mental, spiritual aspect. Wot does this new Age, in which air is the key, the symbol like, wot does it mean to the race on that side?'

'Gas,' interjected the other, but in a lower voice.

From several books lying beside the water-bottle the lecturer selected one. He adjusted a pair of heavy reading-glasses to his eyes.

'The link between the two is better expressed than wot I can express it,' he resumed quickly, 'in this little volume, The New Science of Colour, and colour means light, remember, and light means aether, and aether means space, universality, so it's all the same.'

'Every bit of it,' came the contemptuous comment from the corner.

'Just this short paragraph, I came across it by chance, except that there reely is no chance at all, and it puts it well. It supplies the link. So I'll read it.' He heavily emphasised certain words:

'We are approaching an age of mental telepathy, in which the organism of the race is about to become attuned to the second sense of the earth and to the third element that sustains her, i.e. air, and in which our action and our outlook will alike assume the characteristics of that element, which are elasticity and brilliance.'

He laid down the book, slowly removing the heavy glasses from his nose, and while 'that's no proof was heard to snap from the corner, the other repeated with emphasis of manner, yet lowering his voice at the same time: 'the organism of the race, becoming attuned to air, elasticity and brilliance.'

Fingering his glasses and looking very thoughtful, the speaker kept silence for a minute or so. He drank a few sips of water slowly, while everybody, even the interjector, waited, and those who had been staring at him turned their eyes away from his face, as though embarrassed to watch him drink. He produced a big handkerchief from his coat-tail pocket, wiped his lips, and replaced the handkerchief with some difficulty whence it came. The pause lengthened, but no one stirred. Then the earnest-faced woman near the door touched Wimble on the arm and indicated an empty chair, but Wimble, too absorbed in the proceedings, shook his head impatiently. Joan slipped into it. Joan, he noticed, did not seem interested; the keen attention she had shown at first had left her face, she looked half bewildered and half bored. 'She's too much in it to need explanation,' flashed across him.

The slight shuffling warned the lecturer that the mind of his audience needed holding lest it begin to wander. Picking up a sheet of paper covered with notes, he advanced to the edge of the little platform and cleared his throat.

'As I've been trying to explain,' he began, ''umanity has now reached a crushial moment in its development. The planet we live on belongs to the sun, and the sun has just entered, in 1881, to be igsact, the sign of Aquarius. Aquarius, according to the old Chaldean system, is wot's called an Air Sign, and the new powers waking in us all, coming down into our world now, will be ruled by the element of air. The Age of Pisces, a Water Sign, is just finished and done with. We are entering another period. A new Age is beginning, the Age of Air.' And he glanced about him as though to catch any evidence of challenge.

'What is an Age?' asked a thin voice from the rear. It was not hostile, and heads were turned to find the questioner, but without success.

'An accomplice,' muttered the habitual interrupter to himself. No one noticed the comment, and Wimble, now completely captured by the collective sympathy, even wondered what he meant.

'I'll tell you,' continued the lecturer, and referred to the sheet of notes in his hand. 'I'll tell you again with pleasure.' He emphasised the word 'again.' The glasses were readjusted. With a certain air of mystery, as though he knew far more than he cared to impart, he read aloud, emphasising frequent passages as his habit was, and making here and there effective and semi-theatrical pauses. Behind this cheapness, however, burned obviously a deep sincerity and belief. He deemed himself a prophet, and he knew a prophet's proverbial fate.

'Astronomers tell us that our sun and his fam'ly of planets revolve around a central sun, which is millions of miles distant,' he read slowly, 'and that it requires about 26,000 years to make one revolution.'

Remembering one of his most successful Primers, Wimble sat forward on his chair, all eagerness. Here was what the critic called a 'fact' at any rate.

'This orbit is called the Zodiac,' continued the other, 'and it is divided into twelve signs.' He mentioned them, beginning with Aries and Taurus, and ending with Aquarius and Pisces. 'Now, you asked what is an Age, didn't you?' He paused a second. 'Well, our solar system takes a bit over 2000 years to pass through each of these Signs, and this time is the measurement of an Age. And with each Age certain new things 'appen.'

He made this announcement with a certain mysterious significance.

'Certain things 'appen to the planet and to us as lives on it. Certain changes come. They're sure as summer and winter is sure, that is, you can count on them. Those who know can count on them, prophets and people with inner vision. There you get prophecy and the meaning of prophecy. Vision!' And without a vision the people perish, miss their chances, that is. The seers, the mystics, always know and see ahead, and this end of the Age, and of the world as it's sometimes called stupidly, has been prophesied by many.'

The audience was on tiptoe with anticipation. Each individual possibly hoped that certain personal peculiarities of his own were going to be explained, made wonderful. Wimble was particularly aware of this excitement; it dawned upon him that he was about to receive an explanation, and a semi-scientific explanation too, of his own strange ideas and feelings. He glanced across at Joan. She seemed, to his amazement, asleep; her eyes were closed, at any rate; her attention was not held. He wanted to poke her. He wanted to say 'I told you so,' or rather 'You told me so.' But the speaker had ended his pause, and, to Wimble's delight, was explaining that this movement of the sun passes through the Zodiacal Signs in reverse order, 'precession of the equinoxes,' as it is called, Pisces therefore preceding Aquarius instead of following it. Here was another 'fact' that his Knowledge Primer justified.

The personal anticipation in the audience was not immediately satisfied, however. The speaker intensified it first by a slight delay. Aware that he held the minds before him, he took his time.

'Now, these Signs', lifting his eyes from the sheet of paper and fixing them upon a woman in the front row, who at once showed nervousness, as though she would believe black was white, if only he would stare at some one else, ' these Signs ain't just dead things. They reveal and express and convey intelligent life. They're immense intelligences, they're Zodiacal Intelligences. That's wot they are. The 'ole universe, remember, is alive, and you and I ain't the only living beings in it, nor the 'ighest either. We're not the only bodies. No one can say wot constitoots a body, a living body, nor define it. Our planet is a tuppeny-'alfpenny affair compared to the others, and we're nothing but a lot of hinsects like ants and so forth on it. But if the 'ole universe is alive, and we know it is'

'Hanwell,' interrupted the angry man.

'- each and every part of it must be alive too. And you can't leave out the planets, stars, and suns, the most magnificent bodies, called the 'eavenly bodies, as you know. They're all living bodies. They're the bodies of beings, living beings, but beings far higher than wot we are. And the Zodiacal Signs are 'igher still. They represent functions of the universe, as the ancients knew quite well. They're a kind of intelligence we may call per'aps a Group Intelligence.'

Again he paused a moment. Then, as no interruption came, he went on with greater emphasis than before:

'Now, each of these Zodiacal Intelligences, as the sun, with our little earth alongside, passes through it, rules over its partickler period. With every period we enter a new current of forces. Each period, therefore, of about 2000 years has new Gods, new characteristics, new types of 'uman beings with new tendencies and powers and possibilities in them, a new point of view, if you like to call it so, or, as we Aquarians call it, a new consciousness. Well, the Aquarius Sign just beginning, is an Air Sign. We're getting our new powers, our new point of view and hattitude, our new consciousness from the air.'

In his excitement and deep belief the word 'air' was dangerously near 'hair,' but no one smiled. Perhaps even the critic experienced similar difficulties in his home circle that prevented his noticing it, or caring to take advantage of it if he did.

'I've already referred,' the speaker continued, 'to its effect on the physical plane, new inventions and the like, and 'ow men now navigate the air as fish do the sea, and send their thoughts spinning round the world with the speed of lightning. That's easy enough. I mean, you can all see it for yourselves. The areoplane's a fac' nobody can't get away from, whichever way you take it. But the effect on the spiritual plane is not so simple. It's not so easy to describe, far from it, I admit. When a new mode of consciousness begins to hoperate in men and women, they find difficulty in expressing it. They're puzzled a bit. They don't know where they are with it quite. Those 'oo get it first are called quacks and charlituns, and maybe swindlers too. The slower ones regard them with suspicion, and they may think themselves lucky if they 'ain't stoned or burned alive or crucified as they once was.'

He smiled, and the audience smiled deprecating with him.

'And the chief reason for their difficulty,' he went on, 'is simply this: They 'aven't got the language. Nor the words. That's it. The words describe the experiences of a new type of consciousness don't exist at first. They come later, slowly, gradually. They evolve as the new powers in the race evolve.'

He took his glasses off and wiped them carefully.

'So wot's the result?' he asked. 'Why, this. There's only feeling left. The people that first get the new consciousness feel it in them. But they can't prove it to others because their power is small. And they can't explain it in words, because the words don't exist. So there you are. Only the truth is there too jest the same.'

The challenge in his tone was unmistakable, but no one took it up. The critic was making notes on his cuff and probably had not heard it. Some one coughed, however, and feet shuffled here and there.

'I know it's true, and some of you 'ere in front of me know it's true,' the speaker resumed quickly, his eyes alight and intense conviction in his tone and manner, 'but we can't do more at first than feel it and be glad. All we can do is to show it in our lives. We can live it. We can feel the joy and speed and lightness of the air, and we can live it, show it. We can express it that way, leaving the words to follow in good time. And that's a lot, for example guides the world.'

A murmur of applause greeted the emphatic statement, and Wimble, for one, was tempted to rise on his toes with waving hands and give his confession of faith in no uncertain voice. This railway guard, half quack, half prophet, this man of the people whose knowledge was as faulty as his grammar, had offered the first explanation he had yet heard of his own strange attitude to life and of his experiences since boyhood. This man, similarly, had caught his secret from the air. His exposition might be as exaggerated and wild as the critic suggested, yet it was somewhere true, he felt. The man, owing to his very ignorance perchance, had caught at the skirts of a new and mighty truth that in a century would have become a commonplace, but that at the present moment caused others with better education than himself to talk of Hanwell. Wimble felt this excitement in him, to get up before them all and say that he, too, had felt and tried to live this light, new, swift and spontaneous airy consciousness. The impulse, the generous desire to help, caught at him. Another minute and he might have been on his toes, bearing stammering witness to the truth that was in him. The lecturer himself, however, prevented.

'We stand to-day,' he said, using his notes again, 'upon the cusp of the Aquarian Age. The Piscean Age lies behind us. The Zodiacal Intelligences of that Piscean Age were watery powers and water was its keynote and its symbol. It was the Age of Jesus. Now, listen, please, listen closely, for 'istory bears me out.'

He moved nearer to the edge of the platform, and heads were craned forward to lose no word.

'The sun,' he said, in a lowered tone, 'entered the sign of Taurus in the days of our pre'istoric Adam. That was the Taurian Age. Next came the Arian Age, about the time that Abra'am lived, and with Aries the ram replaced the bull. With the rise of the Roman Empire the sun entered the sign of Pisces, and the Piscean Age began. It took the fish for its symbol. That was the Christian Dispensation with its new outlook and attitude, its new powers, its new type of consciousness. Jesus introduced water baptism, and water became the symbol of purification. It was a watery sign, as I told you. While it lasted, as you'll notice, the last 2000 years, this Piscean Age, with a fish for its symbol, 'as certainly been one of water, and the many uses of that element 'ave been emphasised, and sea and lake and river navigation have been brought to a 'igh degree of efficiency.'

He waited for the impression this was bound to produce. It was evidenced by deep silence, broken only by the rustle of paper and soft garments.

'Jesus Himself referred to the beginning of this Aquarian Age in these words,' he continued solemnly and reverently, 'as you'll find in one of Wisdom Books they don't include in our own Bible:

'And then the man who bears the pitcher will walk forth across an   arc of 'eaven; the sign and signet of the Son of Man will stand   forth in the Eastern sky. The wise will then lift up their heads and know that the redemption of the earth is near.'

He paused significantly. Then he added, his hands raised aloft and his eyes turned toward the ceiling:

'We're already in it, the new Dispensation, the New Age, air.'

'Compressed air,' added the critic, after his long silence.

'Bravo! bravo!' exclaimed Wimble, unable to suppress himself.

'But surely a new Age can only begin in each person individually, and not in any other sense,' put in the thin voice that had spoken once before.

Unperturbed, the speaker repeated with deep emphasis, his eyes and hands still raised aloft:

'And air means spiritual. The Aquarian Age is pre-eminently a spiritual age; and its meaning may now be apprehended by multitudes of people, 'ungry for truth, who will now come, are already coming, into an advanced spiritual consciousness. Our air-bodies is being quickened.'

The last few words seemed to produce a strange effect upon the chief critic. Apparently they enraged him. He fidgeted, half rising from his chair as though about to make a violent speech in reply. In the end, however, he did nothing beyond shrugging his shoulders, with a muttered 'Consciousness indeed! Why, you don't even know the meaning of the word!' He leaned back in his seat, unwilling to stay, yet too annoyed to leave; he resigned himself, keeping his great onslaught perhaps for the close of the meeting. Then, suddenly changing his mind, he leaped to his feet. But the lecturer was before him. In a ringing voice that held his audience and drowned the interruption, he dominated the room. He was about to satisfy the anticipation raised some ten minutes earlier. He took his listeners into his confidence.

'Now, ladies and gentlemen,' he cried, 'or brothers and sisters, as I'd prefer to call you if you've no objection, wot is it we Aquarians means when we talk of air, when we speak of air as the sign of the New Age? We call it spiritual. Wot do we reely mean by that? 'Ow can we show it in our lives? Let us come down to plain words, the language of the street.'

There was again a rustle, as pencils and paper were prepared anew for taking notes.

'It means this, to put it quite plainly, simply: It means living lightly, carelessly, spontaneously, as a bird does, so to speak, 'oose 'ome is air and 'oo works 'ard without taking too much thought. It means living by faith and that means, ' he uttered the next words with great emphasis, 'living by the subconsciousness, by intuition.'

'A bird's heart,' he cried, 'lies in the centre of its body. We must live from the centre too.

'That's the secret, and that's the first sign that you're getting it. There you get the first 'int of this new Aquarian Age, and from the moment we entered it, not so long ago, forty years or so, this idea of the Subconsciousness 'as showed itself as the key-word of the day. It's everywhere already. Even the scientific men 'as got it. Bergson began with 'is intuition, and professors like Frood of Vienna and

Young of Zurich caught on like lightning. William James too, and a 'undred others. Why, it's got down into our poietry and novels, and even the pore old dying pulpits 'ave a smack at it just to try and keep their heads above water.

'To live by your subconscious knowledge, instead of by your slow old calculating reason, means a new, airy way of living. And it's spiritual, I say, because it stands for the beginning of a new knowledge and understanding, and therefore a new sympathy with each other. With everybody! All sorts of powers lie in our subconsciousness, powers of the 'ole race, powers forgotten and powers to come, and it's in touch with greater powers still that so far 'ave been beyond us as a race. All knowledge 'ides there, God.

'And if you rely upon it, it will guide you, and guide you quickly, surely, in a flash. Nor you won't go wrong either, for in your subconsciousness you touch everybody else; we all join on down there, within, and that's where the Kingdom of 'eaven lies, and if you rely upon the Kingdom of 'eaven it will guide you right. We all touch 'ands if you go deep enough, and that means brotherhood, don't it? For it means sympathy, understanding, love. The 'ottentot's your neighbour.'

He stepped back, squaring his shoulders and drawing a deep breath as he surveyed his audience.

'Well, it's only just beginning. Some of us, many of us likely, don't know about it yet, don't feel it. We're only ankle-deep as yet. And those 'oo ain't aware of this great subconscious life, no amount of argument or explanation won't put it into them. A new Age touches individuals first, one 'ere, one there. The end of the world, as some call it, 'appens to each heart alone, as somebody said just now. But it'll come to all in the end. It's coming now. We're in Aquarius, and sooner or later we'll all get into the air and know it. And the new inventions, the new tricks everywhere, as I told you, are paving the way already on the physical plane so that even the hintellectuals and materialists are bound to feel its bigger side before long.

'Air! Why, think of it, and wot a lovely symbol it is! It's everywhere. It flows. Nothing belonging to the sky is stationary. It all moves. Light grows and wanes, wind falls and rises, clouds, birds pass rapidly across it. It 'as nothing rigid about it anywhere. Breath is the first sign of life in your body when you're born, and the breath of the spirit is the first sign of life in your soul when you are born again. And the bird, remember, the natural in'abitant of air, 'as its heart in the centre of its body!

'The subconscious powers, the subconscious life, yes, that's the secret. To rely upon it, live and act by it, means to act with the 'ole world at once and know the 'appiness of brother'ood and love. It means to lose yourself, your little conscious, surface, limited self, in the bigger ocean of the air. 'Itherto it's been called living by faith and prayer. That's all right enough, but it ain't enough. That means touching the subconscious at moments only. We want to touch it always and every minute. In this new Aquarian Age it will be at our fingers' ends, so to speak. The "sub" will disappear. The subconscious will become the conscious. We shall know everything, and everything at once; we shall be everywhere, and everywhere at once.' He raised his voice. 'We shall be ONE, and know that we are ONE. We shall 'ave spiritual consciousness.'

The noise of an overturned chair was heard. Outside the shrill blast of distant factory whistles suggested lunch and food. The critic, pushing hastily past the hushed sitters near him, made his way to the door. As he reached the passage he turned. 'That's the best recipe for hysteria I ever heard,' he cried back, 'and the sooner you're safe in Hanwell, the better for the world!' and vanished.

It was an abrupt and violent interruption, but yet it startled no one; the thread of interest was not broken; a few heads turned to look, and then faced towards the lecturer again. A general sigh was heard, expressive of relief. The audience settled itself more comfortably, and a deeper concentration of interest was felt at once. The removal of the hostile element produced an immediate increase of attentive earnestness. It showed first in the lecturer's face; his eyes grew fixed and steady, his manner more confident, more impressive, and his tone of voice had a more authoritative ring than before.

He leaned forward with an air of mysterious intimacy, as though about to share a secret knowledge he had not dared to divulge before a scoffer. There was a booming note about his voice that thrilled. The charlatan that hides in every human soul slipped out, unconsciously perhaps but unmistakably. It was this, possibly, that affected Wimble as he watched and waited, so eagerly attentive; or, possibly, it was some uncanny anticipation of what he was about to hear. An emotion, at any rate, and one shared by others in the small packed room, rose suddenly in his soul. A little shiver ran down his spine, he shuddered, as once before he had shuddered in Maida Vale.

'Before we close this little meeting,' the deep voice rang, 'and before you go your way and I go mine, per'aps not to come across each other's path again for a tidy while, I want to just say this. It's as well we all should know it, so as we are prepared.'

He fixed his glowing eyes on one of his audience, on Wimble, it so happened, and went on slowly, choosing his words with care and uttering them with a conviction that was not without its impressiveness:

'I want to warn you all, to give you this little word of warning. For I'm led to believe, in fact, I may say it's been given me, that a dying Age, don't die without an effort. An expiring Age, so to say, seeks to prolong its life. With the result that, just before it passes, its characteristics is first intensified. The Powers that have ruled over us for 2000 years make themselves felt with extra strength; and these Powers, seeing that their time is past, are no longer right. They're no longer what we need. Good and right in their time, they now seem wrong, and out of place. They're evil. We see them as evil, any'ow, though they make for good in another way. I don't know if you foller me. Wot I mean is that, when an old Age is passing and a new Age coming to birth, there's conflict.'

There was a renewed rustling, as this sentence was written down on many half-sheets that had so far been blank. But Wimble had no need to make a note of it. He remembered that walk down Maida Vale of several months before, and again the singular shudder passed like a little wind of ice along his nerves.

'Conflict means trouble,' continued the speaker amid a solemn hush, 'and nothing big ever comes to birth without labour and travail and pain. We must expect this pain and travail, and be ready for it. A new 'eaven and a new earth will come, but they won't come easily. They will be preceded by a mighty effort of the old ones to keep going a bit longer first. A 'uge up'eaval, physically and spiritually, will take place first, on the earth, that is, as well as in our 'earts, before we all get caught up to meet the Lord in the air.'

His sentences grew slower and more emphatic, more charged with conviction and with warning. He made privileged communications. There were pauses between his utterances:

'I warn you, I prepare you, so that when it comes you will be ready and prepared, not for yourselves, mind, but so as you may 'elp others wot won't quite realise quite wot it all means.

'For there'll be sacrifice as well.

'There's always a sacrifice when a New Age catches 'old of our old earth, and our old earth will shake and tremble in the re-making, and some of us will shake and tremble too. You'll feel, maybe, that shudder in advance and know what it means. Signs and wonders, men's 'earts failing them for fear, and the instability of all solid things.

'There will be death.

'Death takes its 'undreds, aye, its thousands at a time like that, and many, the best and finest usually, go out before their time, as it seems. But, mark this, they go out, to help!

'There comes in the sacrifice.

'They'll be taken off to 'elp, taken into the air, but taken away from those they leave be'ind.'

His tone grew lower, and a deeper hush passed over the little crowd before him. There was dull fire in his eyes. An atmosphere of the prophet clothed him.

'It's just there,' he emphasised, 'that we, we who know, can 'elp.

'For we know that death is nothing more nor less than slipping back into your own subconsciousness, and so becoming greater and finer and more active, more useful, too, and with grander powers, than we ever 'ad in our limited, imperfect bodies. And we know that this separate life, ended at death, is nothing but an episode in our universal life which death can never put an end to because it is imperishable. We are part of the universe, not of this little planet alone.

'There'll be mourning, but we can 'elp dry their tears; there'll be terror, but we can take their fear away; there'll be loneliness, but we can show them, show 'em by the way we live, that there'll be reunion better than before. We all meet in the sub-consciousness, and know each other face to face. For it means reunion in the air, which is everywhere at once and universal, and stands for that denial of space and time, that spiritual haffirmation, we Aquarians call NOW.'

He held out his hands as in blessing over the intently listening and expectant throng. Gazing above their heads into space, he appeared to concentrate his thoughts a moment. Then his face lightened, as though his mental effort had succeeded.

'After every meeting,' he then went on, but this time in a conversational tone, as friend to friend, the prophet and his flock put aside, 'it is our custom, as you know, to find a carrying-away Sentence. Something you can take away and remember easily. Something that sums up all we've talked about together. Something to keep in your minds and think about every minute of the day until we meet again. Something you can try to live in your daily lives.'

He waited a moment to ensure that all listened closely.

'The sentence I've chosen this time will 'elp you to remember all we've said to-day. It's a symbol that includes the 'ole promise of the air that's so soon to be fulfilled in us.

'I'll now give it out, if yer all ready.'

The expectant, eager, attentive faces were a convincing proof that all were ready and listening attentively.

With a happy and confiding smile, the speaker then pronounced the carrying-away sentence:

'The 'eart of a bird lies in the centre of its body.'

CHAPTER XVI

The carrying-away sentence stuck in Wimble's mind as he journeyed back to the flat on the top of a motor omnibus with Joan, for it expressed a concrete fact, a fact that he could understand. 'The heart of a bird lies in the centre of its body,' he murmured to himself happily. It gave him a secret thrill of joy and wonder. His own heart, thrust to the left though it was, felt ageless. The happy, invincible optimism of the bird was in him. To live from the centre was a neat way of expressing what he had been trying to do for so long, and he had not been far wrong in taking the life and attitude of a bird for his symbol. It meant neglecting the strained, laborious effort of the calculating mind, and leaning for help and guidance upon something bigger, deeper, less fallible than the strutting conscious self. The railway guard labelled it the subconscious, that mysterious region in which every soul is linked to every other soul, involving thus that comprehensive sympathy which is the beginning possibly of brotherhood. He phrased it wildly, but that was what he meant. The bigger self that lay like an ocean behind his separate, personal thought shared everything with every one. The joy, the wisdom of the birds! The elasticity and brilliance of the universal air! The divine carelessness that flows from living at the centre!

'Flow, fly, flow!   Wherever I am, I go;   I live in the air   Without thought or care . . . !'

'Daddy, you mustn't hum in public. It sounds so unusual, and people are staring,' Joan reminded him. 'And you'll forget your hat and leave it behind, if you don't put it on.'

He smoothed his ruffled hair and placed his black billycock upon it.

'So you've woken up at last, have you?' he replied, laughing at her. 'You slept through most of the lecture. What did you make of it, eh?'

She looked at him with a puzzled expression in her soft, bright eyes.

'D'you think it was all nonsense? Was it true, I mean?' he repeated.

'He didn't lie, but he didn't tell the truth,' she said at once. 'Besides, I wasn't asleep. I heard it all.'

'You mean he didn't explain it properly?' he asked.

'It was the wrong way,' she said.

'Ah! words'

'He ought to have danced it,' she said suddenly with decision. 'It's too quick, too flashing for words. I could have shown it to them easily, by dancing it.'

He remembered the amazing ideas her dancing gestures on the roof had once put into him. Then, thinking of the teachers of the world conveying their meaning by dancing and gestures from the pulpits, he chuckled.

'Shall we join the Aquarians?' he asked slyly. 'What do you say to becoming members of their Society?'

She took her answer out of his own mind, it seemed.

'If you belong, you belong. You needn't join. Societies are only cages, Daddy. You're caught and you can't fly on.'

'We could spend the money better, yes,' he mumbled. 'Garden-gloves for mother, a lawn-mower, a hurricane lantern for stormy nights or something'

'Much, much better,' she agreed.

'When once we've found the cottage,' he went on vaguely.

'It's there,' she interrupted instantly. 'Let's get the hurricane lantern. I'd love to choose it with you. May I?'

Wimble looked about him as the heavy vehicle lumbered clumsily along its swaying journey. The soft autumn sunshine of hazy gold lay on the streets, but there was a nip, a sharpness in the air that put an electric sparkle into everything. The solid world was really lighter than it looked. There was a covert brilliance ready to dart forth into swift-rushing flame. He felt the throbbing sheen and rustle in the golden light, and his heart sang with joy above the heavy streets and pavements. He was aware of a point of view that almost denied weight to inert matter, making the dead mass of the universe alive and dancing. This nip and sparkle in the air interpenetrated all these fixed and heavy things, these laborious structures, these rigid forms, dissolving them into flowing, ever-changing patterns of fluid loveliness. He saw them again as powder, the parks and road blown everywhere, the pavements lifted, the walls wide open to the sky. The solid earth became transparent, flooded with light and air. It seemed etherealised. It spread great golden wings towards the blazing sun and limitless sky. Air knew no fixed and rigid forms. Societies, of course, were only cages. He saw the huge cage of the earth blow open. Humanity flew out at last. . . .

'We'll get three, and at once,' he remarked, referring to the lanterns. 'And a pair of hedge-clippers as well, a ladder for the fruit trees, two pair of best garden-gloves for mother, and a revolving summer-house where she can follow the sun and sit in peace.'

That ridiculous lecture acted like some mental cuckoo that had chucked him finally out of the nest into the air. If he did not actually fly, he certainly walked on air, with the same faith that had once been claimed for walking on the sea. He became a daring and a happy soul. Air represented a confident and free imagination in which everything was possible. Earth he still loved, but only as a place to land on and take off from. Imagination and intuition must still, at his present stage, be backed and checked by reason; earth was still there to sleep on. But that spontaneous way of living which is air, using the ground merely as the swallow does, a swallow that exists in space and almost entirely neglects its legs, this careless and new attitude leaped forward in him towards realisation. A bird, he remembered, though apparently so free and careless, works actually with an ordered precision towards great purposes.

He seemed conscious suddenly of a complete and absolute independence, beyond the need of any one's comprehension. Few, if any, would understand him, but that did not matter. The need to be understood was left behind, below. He had soared beyond the loneliness even of a god. He felt very humble, but very happy. And the loneliness would be but temporary, for the rest of the world would follow before long. . . .

The motor omnibus lurched and stopped with grunting noises. Wimble, led by his more nimble daughter, climbed down the narrow spiral stair. He glanced upwards longingly as he descended. He saw the flashing birds. 'The brotherhood of the air,' he thought. 'Oh, how the earth must yearn for it!'

'There's an ironmonger,' cried Joan, pointing across the road. And they went in to buy the hurricane lanterns. They assumed, that is, that the cottage was already found.

Then, after luncheon, while Mother criticised the garden-gloves, observing with regard to the hurricane lanterns that it was 'living backwards, rather, to buy things before we have the place to use them in,' he took from the book-shelf his copy of the Queen of the Air and read once again a favourite passage. It was thumb-marked, the margin scored by his pencil long years ago.

' . . . the bird, in which the breath, or spirit, is more full than in any other creature and the earth-power least. . . . It is little more than a drift of the air brought into form by plumes; the air is in all its quills, it breathes through its whole frame and flesh, and glows with air in its flying, like a blown flame: it rests upon the air, subdues it, surpasses it, outraces it; is the air, conscious of itself, conquering itself, ruling itself.

'Also, into the throat of the bird is given the voice of the air. All that in the wind itself is weak, wild, useless in sweetness, is knit together in its song . . . unwearied, rippling through the clear heaven in its gladness, interpreting all intense passion through the soft spring nights, bursting into acclaim and rapture of choir at daybreak, or lisping and twittering among the boughs and hedges through heat of day, like little winds that only make the cowslip bells shake, and ruffle the petals of the wild rose. . .
.'

His reading was interrupted by the entrance from the passage of his wife, her face heavily veiled; she was dressed for the street, in solemn black; she wore a mysterious yet very confident expression. 'Joe dear, I'm going out. I have an appointment at three o'clock sharp. I mustn't be late.'

He watched her with an absent-minded air for a moment, as though he saw her for the first time almost; all he could remember about her just then was that during the cinema performance she had said with proud superiority: 'I'm glad I'm English.' Then, recognising his wife, he realised that she was going to confession, of course, for he guessed it by the way she folded her hands, waiting patiently for a word of commendation.

'All right, my dear,' he said, 'and good luck. You'll be back for tea, I suppose.' He rose and kissed her on her heavy veil, and she went out with a smile. 'I'm so glad,' he added.

'That's her stage,' he thought to himself, 'and the critic and the Aquarian quack have their stage, and I have mine. It's all right.'

There were immense tracts of experience in everybody, unknown, unused, but waiting to be known and used. Some people lived in one tract only, caged and fixed, unaware of the vast freedom a little farther outside themselves. Different people knew different tracts, each positive that his own particular tract alone was right, as for him, assuredly, it was thinking also that it was the only one, the whole, which, assuredly, it was not. There was, however, assuredly, a point of view, the bird's, that saw all these tracts at once, the boundaries and divisions between them mere walls erected by the mind in ignorance. The bird's-eye view looked down and saw the landscape whole, the divisions unreal, the separation false. This attitude was the attitude of air; air unified; the unity of humanity was realised. Consciousness, focussed hitherto upon little separate tracts with feeble light, blazed upon all at once with shining splendour.

It was true. A great world-telepathy was being 'engendered,' barriers of creed and class were crumbling, democracy was combing out its mighty wings; the 'tracts' inhabited by Mother, Tom, the quack, the critic, by himself and by Joan, by that narrow snob and gossip at the tea-party who asked, 'Who was she?' all these would be seen as adjoining little strips belonging to the universal air which knows neither strips, divisions nor boundaries.

A great light blazed into his heart. He wondered. Apparently it was the little, simple, insignificant people, and not the great minds of the day, who were the first to become aware of air. The great ones were too rigid. Air rushed first into the hearts of the uneducated, the ignorant, the unformed and informal, the little children of the race. It has been ever so. The learned, knowing too much, solid with facts and explanations, are no longer fluid. They neither flow nor fly. The brotherhood of air, he grasped, would come first through the untaught babes and little children of earth's vast, scattered family.

And, while these vague reflections danced across his mind, dropping their curious shadows upon his own little tract of experience, his wife was whispering her sins to another mind who should forgive them for her, the critic was writing a vehement pamphlet to prove that he alone was right, Tom, in the office, was scheming new plans for making money that should satisfy his natural desires for pleasure and self-indulgence, the quack was elaborating Zodiacal Explanations in his studio next to his Private Consulting Room, and Joan

He listened. A light, tripping step went down the corridor, passed his door and began to climb the ladder to the open skylight in the hall. He listened closely, eagerly, a new rhythm catching at his heart. The little song came to him faintly through the obstructing barriers of brick and mortar. He caught the tap and tremble of her feet upon the roof.

Joan sang and danced above the world.

CHAPTER XVII

'Careless as a bird! Bird-happy and bird-wise,' he murmured to himself as they moved in a month later. For he had found a cottage as by instinct. It was not on the agents' list of modern, ugly and comfortless cages, but was an old-world little place that had caught his eye by the corner of the lane as he returned to the country station, weary and almost faith-less, after a vain inspection. A white board suddenly peered at him through the branches of a yew, there were roses up the walls, a tiny fountain played on the lawn, and beyond he caught a glimpse of a neglected orchard, sloping fields of yellow ragwort, and a stream. The stream, moreover, ran under the road just there, so that he could look down into it from the old stone bridge. The water ran swiftly, but deep enough to grow long weeds of green and gold that swung with the current like thick fairy hair. Two or three silver birches shone and rustled by the wicket-gate. He went in. A robin hopped up, inspected him, and hopped away into the shadow of the yew.

The interior seemed to him like a bit of forest, the beams, the panelling, the dark, stained settles. Yet there was a bathroom, too, the kitchen was large and light, the bedrooms airy, the living-rooms just right in size and number. The front windows looked out across the rose-plot to the little green where the geese were gabbling, while the back ones opened straight into the orchard, where fruit and walnut trees stood ankle deep in uncut grass. The windows, too, were wide and high, letting in big stretches of the sky. Also, there were a mulberry-bush and several heavy quince trees. And the stream ran singing and bubbling between the orchard and the farther fields, where, amid the sprinkled gold of the ragwort, scuttled countless rabbits.

Moreover, it was cheap, the drains were safe, the church was as picturesque as an old-fashioned Christmas card, and the vicar was brother to a peer. Thus there was something for everybody. The nest was found. Mother inspected it in due course and gave her modified approval; Tom said it 'sounded ripping,' he would 'run down for week-ends' whenever he could; and Joan, catching her breath when she saw it first on the afternoon of a golden-brown October day, felt a lump in her throat and moisture in her eyes, such happiness rose in her breast. She stood with her father in the sandy lane, Mother had gone inside at once, the larches rustling and the excited geese examining their stiff town clothing from behind. On the topmost branch of an apple tree a big brown thrush was singing its heart out over the garden, its small packed outline silhouetted against the pale blue sky. Joan caught her father's hand.

'Look!' she whispered, pointing. 'Listen!'

He did so. He felt the strange excitement in the child. Her lips were parted and her shining eyes turned heavenwards a moment. The thrush poured forth its liquid song deliciously; and the sound sank into his heart as though it expressed the full happiness of the air that welcomed them to the cottage and the garden. He experienced surely something of the soft air-magic as he stood there watching, listening. The natural joy and sweetness of it touched him deeply. And his daughter sang a strange thing then, murmuring it to herself. He only just caught the curious words:

'There's a bird for me   On the apple tree!   It's explaining all the garden!'

Up the scaffolding of the quaint phrases he passed, as it were, with her into the clear air beside the singing bird: that scrap of nonsense 'explaining all the garden' did the trick. A sack of meanings seemed emptied before him out of the sweet October sky. The interesting, valuable ideas in life began, he realised, just where language stops, intelligible, sensible language, that is. Then came either poetry, legend, nonsense, or else mere silence. Joan used a combination of the former.

'Words are parvenu people,' he recalled a Primer sentence, 'as compared with thought and action. Communications between God and man must always be either above or below them; for with words come in translations.'

'Explaining all the garden!' The touch of nonsense brought a thousand 'translations' into his mind. The air was full of fluttering meanings that showered about him. He balanced aloft on the twig beside the singing thrush, his sight darting, as with the bird's-eye view, upon recent happenings. He read various translations instantaneously.

In front of him stood the cottage and garden, the fields and trees and stream he had dreamed about with his daughter, an accomplished, solid fact. It had come as by magic, materialised by thought and desire, and yet, as Mother said, 'by chance.' But the chance included method, because Fate obeyed a confident Belief. And circumstances were moulded or modified by faith. He and Joan somehow held the sure sweetness of fulfilment in their minds from the beginning; they had always believed, indeed had known, the cottage would be found. And it had been found. He had not fussed nor worried; there had been no friction due to the grit of doubt. Like his queer, spontaneous daughter, he had believed in his dream, and at the same time kept his eyes wide open like a hawk.

As he stood there, listening to the song of the thrush and aware of its poise on the swaying twig balanced so steadily, yet alert for spontaneous flight in any direction, these fluttering translations of the child's nonsense words shot through him. The joy of the happy thrush shone in his heart, explaining the garden that was life.

The bird, at that moment, flew off with a whirr of wings, still singing as it vanished with an undulating swoop over the roof towards the orchard. Across the patch of watery blue sky he had been watching shot half a dozen swallows, then intent only upon darting insects, although on the eve of their huge journey of ten thousand miles. Beyond them two plover tumbled like blown leaves towards the ground, yet rising again instantly before they touched it . . . and into his hand he felt Joan's fingers creep softly. He looked down into her eyes, moist with excitement, joy, and wonder. The magic of the air seemed all about them, in their minds and hearts and very bodies even.

'You've found a real nest, Daddy, but we can travel everywhere from here.' It was said simply, as though a bird had learned to speak. 'Think of the journeys we shall make, just by staying here!'

'The cottage seems swung in the branches, doesn't it?' he replied. 'Come on, now; let's go inside.' And he walked across the lawn, lifting his feet quickly, lightly, as though he feared his weight might hurt the earth, yet still more as though he might any instant spring into the air and follow the thrush, the plover, or the swallows.

Upon the threshold of the open door, at that minute, Mother faced them. Having made her inspection of the arrangements and the furniture, all that the workmen had done in the last few days, she came out to report. She stood there very solidly, her feet in goloshes, planted tenaciously upon the damp October earth. She was smiling contentedly; behind her gleamed the white apron of the parlourmaid. Tea obviously was ready and she was waiting for them to come in. A fire burned pleasantly in the dining-room, glinting on a clean white table-cloth. There were buttered toast and a jug of cream, solid realities both. This atmosphere of wholesome, earthly comfort glowed about her. Her very smile conveyed it.

'Mother's settled down already,' Joan whispered. 'She likes it! That means Tom'll like it too. But she'll live indoors.'

In his own mind, however, rose another thought, although he agreed with what she said. He was thinking how odd it was that Mother always appeared to be settled in the mouth of a hole. She stood, framed by the dark doorway, as though a deep burrow stretched behind her and below. The simile of the nervous badger, peering forth upon a dangerous upper world, passed through him. A great tenderness rose in his heart. Mother, he knew, though she had done no actual work, had felt the move a heavy strain. To dig a new hole, of course, was a dusty and laborious job, whereas to flutter across a few fields to another tree was but a careless joy.

'I've been through all the rooms,' she said cautiously, as they went down the passage, 'and everything seems very nice indeed, Joe. The wood makes it seem a bit dark, perhaps, but it's all very respectable. And the parlour looks really quite distinguished. Tea's laid for us in the dining-room.'

They went in; the fire shone brightly; the lamp was lit. Mother moved towards the great silver tea-pot, letting herself down with a sigh into the black horsehair arm-chair. It was as though she went down into the earth. He sat with his cup of tea in the wide settle of the ingle-nook, and Joan, having first seen to her parents' wants, then took the corner facing him.

They settled in. Yet this settling was characteristic of the family, for whereas Mother settled down, Mr. Wimble and his daughter became unsettled. That is, they felt restless. Mother, with the security of a comfortable home and comfortable income at her back, cropped her food safely, yet wondered why she felt dull and bored and lonely. There is no call to describe the actions and reactions of her familiar type to the conditions of the quiet country life, and her chief tragedy that winter was perhaps that when 'his lordship, the vicar,' called, he surprised her in old garden clothes, the fire in the 'distinguished parlour' (kept unused against just this particular event) unlighted, so that she was obliged to receive him in the dark dining-room with the ungentlemanly settles.

Joan and her father were unsettled for the very reason that made her settled. Mother felt her feet. They felt their wings.

A week after the settling in, their restless feeling, wholly unanticipated, came to a head. The windy skies were already calling the swallows together swiftly, collecting their mobile squadrons in a few hours for the grand southern tour. And these amazing birds seemed nothing less than an incarnation of the air itself. There is nothing of earth about them anywhere; their feet are too weak to stand on the ground; every darting turn they make is a movement of the entire creature, rather than of the head first and then the body; they have no necks, their bullet heads turn simultaneously with the tail, and all at once. Joan and her father watched them daily going about their careless, windy life, gathering on the telegraph wires, giving the young ones hints, on the wing to the very last minute. They had no packing-up to do.

'They'll be off soon now,' said Joan. 'Wherever they are, they go, don't they?' There was a tinge of restless desire in her eyes as she followed their movements.

'A few days, yes,' said her father. 'About the middle of the month they leave. They know right enough.'

And two days later, it was October 15th, Joan woke at dawn and looked out of her open window. The twittering of many thousand voices had called her out of sleep, but something in her heart had called her too. It was very early, the daylight of dawn, yet not the daylight quite, and everywhere, from fields and trees, the chorus of bird-life was audible. Birds sing their best and loudest always in that half-hour which precedes the actual dawn. The volume is astonishing. 'As the real daylight comes, it sinks and almost ceases, and never in the whole twenty-four hours is there such an hour again.' The entire air seemed calling 'good-bye and safe return' to those about to leave.

Joan ran and woke her father. 'They're off,' she whispered, as he crawled out of his warm bed, careful not to waken his wife. 'Come and say good-bye.'

The peculiar joy and mystery of early morning was in the quiet house and in the sharp tang of the fresh, cool autumn air. In nightgown and pyjamas, a single rug about their shoulders, they leaned out of the upper window. The ivy rustled just beneath them on the wall, there was a whisper among the yellow walnut leaves to their right, the orchard trees hung still and motionless, breathing out the perfume of earth and fruit and heavy dew.

The sky, however, was alive; it seemed all motion; even the streaky clouds tinged with pale colour looked like stretched wings mightily extended. And the vague murmur of a flock of birds rose everywhere. There was a hurricane of wings above the world, as the armies of the swallows came carelessly together. They left in scattered groups, but with every party that left, another instantly assembled, born out of empty space. Multitudes took the wing towards the sea, while other darting multitudes collected instantly behind them. The air, indeed, was alive and whirring into a symbol of lovely, rushing flight, swarming, settling, turning, wheeling in a turmoil of ascending and descending feathers that yet expressed a design of ordered beauty. Myriad clusters formed, then instantly dispersed again, threaded together upon one invisible pattern; now herded into a wedge, shaped like a wild black comet, now circling, streaming, dividing, melting away into a living cloud. The evolutions were bewildering.

As the eastern horizon began to burn with red and gold, the wings took colour faintly, brightening as an upward slant revealed their pallid under-sides, then darkening again as they tilted backwards. The swallows alternately focussed and dispersed. Separate hordes, turning at high velocity with one accord, shot forth and away to the south. They rose, they sank, they vanished. They went first to the coast; for their migration, led by the infallible sense of orientation which is subconscious knowledge, takes place chiefly in the night, in darkness. Within a brief half-hour the whole of the immense army disappeared. The sky was still and silent, motionless and empty. The swallows were gone.

'They've taken part of me with them,' whispered Joan, 'part of my warmth,' and she drew the rug closer about her shoulders as the October sun came up above the misty fields.

'They'll be in Algeria to-morrow,' sighed her father, 'and I'd like to be there too.' His thought went back to the sun-drenched garden where nightingales sang in the February moonlight. . . . The old romance stirred in him painfully. 'Mother, poor old Mother,' he murmured to himself, 'she seemed so wonderful then. How strange!' He felt himself old suddenly. He felt himself caught, caged, stuck.

'That's where I was born, wasn't it?' Joan asked, catching the sentence. She straightened herself suddenly, throwing the rug aside; the sun shone into her face and on her golden hair that fell rippling over her nightgown. The light gleamed, too, in her moistened eyes. He saw joy steal back upon her. 'But, Daddy,' she exclaimed with an odd touch of confident wonder in her voice and look, 'we can be there just the same, if we want to.' She raised herself on her toes a moment as though she were going to dance or fly. In the pale gold light of the sunrise she looked like some ethereal bird of fire rising into the air.

'We can be everywhere, everywhere at once, really! Don't you see? We always want to be somewhere else anyhow. That proves it.'

And as she said it, he remembered the cinema, and felt his wings again; he was free, uncaged; of course he could go anywhere, everywhere at once almost. He knew himself eternally young. He realised Air, that which is everywhere at once and cannot age. Earth obeys time, grows old, changes, and eventually dies; but air is ever changeless, free of time altogether, unageing. It cannot wear away, it is invisible, omnipresent. The wings of the spirit opened in him, rose into space and light, then flashed, darting after the amazing swallows. 'Wherever I am, I go,' he hummed, as he went softly back along the cold passage and crept cautiously into bed beside his wife, who, heavily breathing still, had not moved since he left her, and lay in ignorance of the sunrise, as also of the army of happy wings that by now were already out of England and far across the sea.

And, later in the day, as he stood with her near a gravel-pit beside the road, watching a colony of busy starlings, she objected: 'What a noise and fuss about nothing! What a nuisance they are, Joe.

Do come on, dear. There's really nothing to watch, and I want to get in and change my things in case any callers come.'

He remembered a passage about starlings written by a strenuous big-game hunter, who yet had the air-magic in his blood. He quoted it to her, as best he could, and she said it was pretty:

'Happy birdies! What a bore all morality seems, as one watches them. How tiresome it is to be high in the scale (and human)! Those who would shake off the cobwebs, who are tired of teachings and preachings and heavy-high novellings, who would see things anew, and not mattering, rubbing their eyes and forgetting their dignities, missions, destinies, virtues, and the rest of it, let them come and watch a colony of starlings at work in a gravel-pit.'

'Yes,' he agreed, 'quite pretty. Selous got a glimpse there, didn't he? but only a glimpse. The great thing is to see it all. He forgot the swallows.'

His thought ran on, fragments becoming audible sometimes. 'It's all one, you see. Stars and starlings are the same one thing, only differently expressed. . . . That's what genius does, of course. Genius has the bird's-eye point of view. . . . It sees analogies everywhere, the underlying unity of everything, sees the similar in the dissimilar. It reduces the Many to the One,' he added in a louder tone, as a Primer came opportunely to his support.

'I ask you, Mother,' he cried with enthusiasm, 'what else is genius but that? I ask you?'

'What?' said Mother, as they went indoors.

CHAPTER XVIII

Wimble watched the year draw to its close and run into the past. Born slowly out of sullen skies, it had shaken off the glistening pearls of April and slipped, radiant and laughing, into May; at the end of June, full-bosomed still and stately, it had begun to hasten, lest the roses hold it prisoner for ever; pausing a moment in August, it looked out with perfect eyes upon the world as from a pinnacle; then, poised and confident, began the grand descent down the red slopes of Autumn into the peace of winter and the snow.

Thus, at least, its history described itself in Wimble's thoughts, because his little mind, standing on tiptoe, saw it whole and from above. 'You ought to publish it, dear,' said Mother, to whom he mentioned it one December evening round the fire. 'You really ought to write it.' He objected that everybody knew it just as well as he did. 'It's always happening to everybody, so why should I remind them?' 'Because they don't see it,' was her answer. 'Besides, they'd think you wonderful.' But Wimble was no writer. He shook his untidy head, yet secretly pleased with his wife's remark that people don't see the obvious. It was almost an air-remark. Mother was changing a little. . . . And he dozed in his chair, thinking how easily the world calls a man wonderful, he has but to startle it, and how easily, too, that man is destroyed if he believes its verdict.

With the rare exception of occasional signs like this, however, his wife had not mobilised her being radically for a big change. She retired into her prosaic background, against which, as with certain self-protecting, ultra-cautious animals and insects, she remained safely invisible. Back to the land proved rather literal for her; she wore her heavy garden-gloves with pride. At the same time her practical nature, streaked with affection, patience, and unselfishness, took on, somehow, a tiny glint of gold. Her eyes grew lighter, her movements less laborious. Fear lessened in her; joy often caught her by surprise. Sparks, though not yet flame, lit up her attitude to things, as if, close to her beloved element of earth, the country life both soothed and blessed her. She felt at home. She said 'what' far less frequently. This quiet, peaceful winter was perhaps for her a period of gestation. The family gathered about her more than in town.

With a buoyancy hard to define and possibly not justified, Wimble watched her. He looked out upon life about him. His health was good, but this buoyancy was based on something deeper than that; his health was good because of it. Nothing mattered, a foolish phrase of those who shirked responsibilities, was far from him; everything mattered equally expressed it better. The New Thing coming, which he and Joan called Air, lay certainly in him, though very far yet from finding full expression. The germ of it at any rate lay in him, as in her. The fact that they recognised it was proof of that. A divine carelessness took charge of his whole life and being; Mother was aware of it; even Tom responded mildly: 'quite sets a fellow up,' as he expressed it after his rare week-end visits, the Sunday spent in killing rabbits; 'town's overrated after all.'

They merged pleasantly enough with their surroundings, melting without shock into the life of neighbours, sharing the community existence, narrow, conventional, uninspired though it was. And all through the dark and clouded months, the skies emptied of birds, weighted at the low horizons, afraid to shine, yet waiting for the marvellous coming dawn, all through these heavy weeks and days Joan's presence, flitting everywhere with careless singing and dancing, shot the wintry gloom with happy radiance. It was her spontaneous dancing that especially made Wimble stare and wonder. It conveyed meanings no words could compass, expressing better than anything else the new attitude he felt coming into life. He remembered the flood of shadowy ideas her graceful gestures had poured into him once before when he walked up Maida Vale; and that strange night in the flat when, seeing her dancing on the London roof, he was dimly aware of a new language which included even inanimate objects. The strange shudder that accompanied the vision he had forgotten.

This magical rhythm was her secret. It stirred the heart, making it vulnerable to impulses from some brighter, happier state she knew instinctively and in advance. Mother, he noticed, watched her too, peering above her knitting-needles, moving her head in sympathy, sometimes a faint, wondering smile lighting upon her bewildered, careworn face. A real smile, however, for it was in the eyes alone, and did not touch the lips. Even Tom admired. 'You ought to be taught,' he said guardedly. 'You'd touch 'em up a bit. If you did that in church the whole world would go.' He too, without knowing it, realised that something sacred, inspired, regenerating was being whispered.

Yet Joan herself, though growing older, hardly developed in the ordinary way. She did not grow up. She remained backward somehow. She lived subconsciously, perhaps. Some new knowledge, gathering below the surface, found expression in this spontaneous dancing. With the dawn, now slowly coming, it would burst full-fledged upon the world, and the world itself would dance with joy. Meanwhile, a new bloom, a new beauty settled on the girl, and Mother proudly insisted that she 'must go to a good photographer and have her picture taken.' But the result was commonplace, for in the rigid black and white outline all the subtlety escaped, and, regretting the money wasted, Mother wondered why it had failed. Like the audience at the Vicarage charities when Joan danced, she watched the performance, felt a hint of strange beauty, clapped her hands and wondered 'what it meant.'

'It's her life, you see,' Wimble comforted her. 'And you can't photograph life. To get her real meaning, we ought to do it with her, dance it.'

'She's light, rather, for her age,' replied Mother ambiguously. 'But everybody seems to love her somehow,' she added proudly. 'She seems to make people happy. P'r'aps later she'll develop and get sensible.' She sighed, and resumed her knitting. Presently she got up to light the lamps. 'The days are drawing out, Joe,' she mentioned, smiling. 'Spring will be here before we know it.' He lifted the chimney to help her, turned up the wick, struck a match, and kissed her fondly.

The country life, it seemed, had brought them all together more, made them aware of their underlying unity, as it were. They flocked. Wimble, dressed now in wide brown knickerbockers, wearing bright stockings and brogue shoes with feathered tongues that flapped when he walked, noticed the change with pleasure. The new attitude was only in his brain as yet, but it was already stealing down into his heart. This increased sense of a harmonious manifold unity in the family impressed him, and it was Joan, he felt, who made him see it, if she was not also the cause of its coming to pass. Only some spiritual actuary could make it quite clear, but he discerned the oneness behind the different members of his family, uniting them. In this subconscious, completer self lay full understanding. There was no need to pay annual subscriptions to an Aquarian Society to realise that! Moreover, if a small family with such divergent interests and ambitions could flock and realise unity, the larger family of a village, country, nation could do the same, once the underlying unity were realised. That was the difficulty. The whole world was, after all, but a single family, humanity. . . . In his quiet country nook Wimble dreamed his great dream. He saw the nations with but a single flag, a single drum, a single anthem, true to a larger single patriotism that could never again be split up into lesser divisional patriotisms. The universal fraternity of indivisible Air was coming; the subconscious where individuals pooled their surface differences would become conscious; that was the truth, he felt, the one great thing the Aquarian lecturer had said. . . . He remembered the cinema, with its mechanical suggestion of a unification of world-experience faintly offered; he remembered the free, happy, collective life of the inhabitants of air, the natural singers of the world. The deep underlying sense of unity buried in the subconscious once realised, full understanding must follow, and with complete understanding the way was cleared for love. And it was Joan's dancing, somehow, that set the dream within his heart. The new attitude to life he imagined dawning on the world was the first hint of a coming spiritual consciousness, and for spiritual consciousness the totality of things is present. 'All at once and everywhere at once,' as she had put it. His heart swelled big within him as he dreamed. . . .

'Coal's getting very expensive,' mentioned Mother, as she leaned forward beside him to poke the fire. 'We'd better mix it with coke. You might find out, Joe. We can't go on at this rate.'

'I will, dear,' he replied. 'I'll write to Snodden and Tupps at once.' He patted her knee and got up to go to his little den where he kept his papers, books, and pipes, reflecting as he did so that it was easy enough to love the world; it was loving the individual that breaks the heart. Pricked by an instant of remorse, then, it occurred to him that a pat on the knee, as a sign of love, might be improved. He trotted back and kissed her. 'We must flock more and more and more,' he mumbled, and before she could say 'What, Joe?' he gave her another kiss and was gone to write to his coal merchant as she had suggested. He would bring back the bird into Mother's heart or die in the attempt. If the new thing he dreamed about didn't begin at home, it was not worth much. He felt happy, so happy that he longed to share it with others; he would have liked to mention it in his letter to the coal merchant. Instead, he merely began, 'Dear Messrs. Snodden and Tupps,' yet signed himself, 'Yours full of faith,' since 'faithfully' alone sounded insincere.

'Odd,' he reflected, 'that unless happiness is shared, it's incomplete, unsatisfying. The chief item lacks. Selfish happiness is a contradiction in terms. We are meant to share everything and be together more. There's the instinctive proof of it.' If the coal merchant felt equally happy, he might even have shared his coal. 'But he'd only think me mad if I suggested that,' thought Wimble, chuckling. 'We can exchange coal and money and still love one another.' He posted the letter before he could change his mind, and came back to his wife. 'Some day,' he said, as he sat down and poked the fire, 'some day, Mother, and not very far off either, we shall all be sharing everything all over the world, just as birds share the air and worms and water.' This time she did not ask him to repeat his words. She smiled a comfortable smile half-way between belief and incredulity. 'You really think so, Joe?' 'It's coming,' he rejoined; 'it's in the air, you know, for I feel it. Don't you?' he added. He leaned nearer and softly whispered in her ear, 'You're happy here, aren't you, Mother? Much happier than you used to be? 'She smiled again contentedly. 'The country air, Joe dear,' she replied. 'The bird's flown back into you,' he said, taking her hand and ignoring the bunch of knitting-needles that came pricking with it. 'Perhaps,' she mumbled, 'perhaps. Life's sweeter, easier than it used to be, in some ways.' She flushed a little, while Wimble murmured to himself, yet just low for her to hear, 'and in your heart some late lark singing, dear. A new thing is stealing down upon us all.' 'There's something coming, certainly,' she agreed. 'Come,' he corrected her, 'not coming. It's here now.' Holding hands, they looked into each other's eyes, as Joan's little song and dancing steps went down the passage just outside.

CHAPTER XIX

January sparkled, dropped like a broken icicle, and was gone; February, so eager for the sun that she shortens her days while lengthening her searching evening hours, summoned one night the tyrant winds of March; these shouted and blew the world awake, then yielded with a sigh to the kiss of April's laughter. A disturbing sweetness ran upon the world, agitating the hearts and minds of men. Yearning stirred even among deep city slums; in the country hope and desire burst into glad singing. Spring returned with her eternal magic. The hawthorn was in bloom.

The birds came back, filling the air with song, with the glance of wings and the whirr of feathers, with the gold and confidence of coming summer. The air was alive again with careless joy. Wimble responded instantly. The thrill pierced to his very marrow. Memories revived like wild-flowers, and his thoughts, shot with the gold and blue of lost romance, turned to the open air. He got some sandwiches, mounted his bicycle, and, followed by Joan, started in a southerly direction as once, long years ago, he had escaped from streets and lectures to spend a day with his beloved birds. This time, however, it was not the willow-haunted Cambridge flats that were his aim. He took Joan with him to the bare open downs above the sea.

It was a radiant morning, and a south-west wind blew gently in their faces. Wimble's felt hat fluttered behind him at the end of a string, as they skimmed down the sandy lanes towards Lewes, the smooth, scooped hollows of the downs coming nearer every minute. Their majestic outline seemed hung down from the sky itself, yet in spite of their mass they had a light, almost transparent look in the morning brilliance. They melted into the air. The noble line of them flung upwards the space as though time met eternity and disappeared.

Down the long hill into the ancient town Joan shot past him. He noticed her balance, and thought of the perfect equilibrium of a bird that shoots full speed upon its resting-place, then stops, securely poised, making no single effort to recover steadiness. For all its tiny legs, no bird wobbles or overbalances, much less trips or stumbles. Joan flew ahead of him, both hands off the bars. The careless gesture reminded him of the matchless grace of the wagtail. He laughed aloud, coasting after her unconscious ease with his own more deliberate, reasoned caution. 'She could fly to Africa without a guide!' he thought, aware for an instant of the great subconscious rhythm in Nature birds obeyed instinctively. No wonder their purposes were carelessly achieved. 'She's sure,' he added. 'Something very big takes care of her, and she knows it.'

They walked up the steep hill out of the town, ran to the left along a chalky lane, dipped in between the folds of grassy hills and great covering fields, Joan leading always without hesitation. Once they paused to watch the aerial evolutions of a body of plover, rising, falling, tumbling, turning at full speed without confusion or collision, as though one single telepathic sympathy operated throughout the entire mass of individuals. Instinct the Primers called it, but Wimble, recalling the Aquarian lecture, caught at another phrase, subconscious unity. It was a power, at any rate, beyond man's conscious reasoning mind. The careless safety of the birds amazed him. 'Air wisdom!' he exclaimed aloud to Joan; 'we shall all have it some day!' It was odd how that crazy lecture had lodged ideas in his thoughts, claiming confirmation, returning again and again to his memory. They coasted down a grassy track into a village, left their bicycles behind a farmer's gate, and sat down a moment to recover breath. It was ten o'clock in the morning.

From the tiny hamlet, where a few flint cottages and barns clustered about an ivied church, they took the path southwards up the slope. In the cup or the hills below them sheltered the toy buildings and the trees. The rooks, advertising their clumsy flight and semi-human ways, cawed noisily, playing in the gusty wind. They showed off consciously, devoid of grace. One minute the scene was visible below, a perfect miniature; the next it was hidden by a heavy shoulder of ground; the earth had swallowed it, church, houses, trees, and all. No sound was audible. Even the rooks had vanished. In front stretched an open and a naked world. The human couple paused a moment and stared. The wind went past their ears. There was a sense of immensity and freedom. There was great light. They were on the Downs.

'Oh, Daddy,' cried Joan, 'we're out of England! This is the world!'

'And the world has blown wide open!' he replied. 'I feel everywhere at once!' The gust whirled his words and laughter into space. 'The misunderstanding of streets and houses leaves' he snatched at the same time at his vanishing hat and seized the cord.

Joan flung herself backwards against the wind with arms spread out, her hat in one hand and a blue-ribbon that had tied her hair fluttering in the other. The loosened hair streamed past her neck, great strands of it flattened against the curve of her back as well, her short skirts flapping with a noise like sails. Then, turning about, she faced the gust, and everything streamed the other way. The wind clapped the clothes so tight against her slender figure that it seemed to undress her, or rather made them fit as tight and neat as feathers. Like some bird of paradise, indeed, she looked, the slim black legs straining to take the air. She began to dance.

And as he watched the golden hair against the blue, there flashed into him the memory of a distant day, when a saffron scarf had set his heart on fire with strange airy yearnings, and the blue and golden earth had danced to the tune of another spring. The tiny human outline amid this vast expanse seemed wonderful, so safe, so exquisite, caught in some rhythm born of the immensities of sky and earth and ocean. A mile to the southward lay the sea. There was a taste of clover-honey, a tang of salt, and the gorse laid its sweetness in between the two. Memories crowded upon him as he watched Joan playing and dancing. The fervour and earnestness of her pleasure exhilarated him. 'Blithe creature,' he said to himself, 'you were surely born to fly!' and remembered Mother as she once had been and as she was now. Why had it all left her, this joyous rapture of their early days together? Had the bird flown really from her heart and into Joan? Was it not merely caged awhile? Had he himself not helped to cage it? He recalled her radiant face beside the pond among the emerald Cambridge fields, and the old first love poured back upon him in a flood.

In a lull of the wind he caught the ecstatic singing of a lark, and at the same moment Joan danced back to his side suddenly and seized his arm. Her voice, it almost seemed, carried on the trill and music of the lark. 'It's all new as gold,' she cried. 'Everybody'd live for ever up here. We must bring Mother. She'd flow fly flow all over!'

'Dance, my child,' he exclaimed, 'don't talk! Go on with your dancing. It gives me ideas.'

'But you're always thinking,' she said, still breathless from her exertions. 'It spoils everything, that thinking and thinking'

'It's not thinking,' he interrupted, 'it's seeing. When you dance I see things. I see everything at once. It's like a huge vision, yet so small and simple that it's all in my head at once. It explains the universe somehow to me. Thinking indeed! Why, I never thought in my life'

'There's a bird for me, On the apple tree, It's explaining all the garden,' sang the girl, dancing away towards the yellow gorse. Her father's words conveyed no meaning to her; she had not listened. He watched her. Her movements, he felt, obeyed the great unconscious rhythm that breathes through nature, through the entire universe, from the spinning midge to the most distant sun. Surely it must include humanity as well, these millions of separate individuals who had lost it temporarily, much as Mother had lost the 'bird.' He, too, was caught along with it, as though he shared it, did it, danced it. He could see what he could not say. He understood. Immense, yet at lightning speed, the meaning of Air slid with that simple dancing deep into his heart. It was unity of life everywhere that he saw interpreted, and the ease, the grace, the carelessness were due to their being mothered and inspired by Nature's great safe rhythm. Relying on this, as birds did, there was safety, unerring intelligence, infallible guidance, flight from Siberia to Abyssinia possible without a leader. Birds migrated at night, he remembered, stopping at dawn to rest and sing, then going on again in the twilight: surer of their inner guidance in the darkness than in the blaze of daylight. Amazing symbol! Instinct, unconscious, subconscious, whatever it might be called in rigid language, this deep attitude, poised and steady, obeyed the mighty rhythm that realised the underlying unity of all that lives, of everything. Thought breaks this rhythm, which it should merely guide; reason reduces, opposes, and finally interrupts it. His backward child, and she was still a child for all her eighteen years, had somehow tapped it.

'Dance, my child, dance on!' he cried as he followed her. 'You dance joy and brotherhood into my heart.' And, looking more like a mechanical gollywog than a human being who has discovered truth, he floundered after her as a gnome might chase a butterfly. Thus, swinging along between the yellow gorse, over the tumuli, leaping the rabbit holes, he realised that the love and joy he sought and dreamed about was here and now; not in some future Golden Age, but at his very feet upon the earth. All that he meant by Air and the Airy Consciousness was now. This little prophet without a lyre saw it clear. Torn by the brambles, tripped by the holes, he chased his marvellous dream as once, years before, he had chased an elusive streak of gold across the Cambridge flats. He was caught by the elemental rhythm of the Downs, borrowed in its turn from the suns of uttermost space that equally obeyed and shared it.

He looked about him. Immense domed surfaces, smooth as a pausing ocean, stretched undulating to dim horizons; air lifted the earth into immaterial space; they intermingled; and sight roved everywhere without a break. Upon this vast expanse there were no details to enchain attention, blocking the rhythm of the eye; no points of interest stood up, as in mere 'scenery,' to fasten feeling to a limited area. Enjoyment soared, unconfined, on wings. He saw no barriers, no trees, no hedges or divisions; no summits startled him with 'See, how big I am!' all self-asserting items lacked. Wind, sky, and sea offered their unconditioned, limitless invitation. Even the flowers were unobtrusive, the ragwort, thyme, and yellow gorse claimed no deliberate notice, and the thistle-down flew past like air made visible. It was, in a word, this liberation from detail, snapping attention with definite objects, that set him free in mind, as Joan already proved herself free in action. Earth here was sublimated into air.

'Good heavens!' his heart cried out. 'It's here, it's now, this new thing coming from the Air!'

This deep rhythm of the landscape caught his very feet, making even his physical movements elastic, springy, sharing the rise and fall of flight expressed in the waving surface of the world about him. He no longer stumbled. Joan's dancing, though apparently she merely leapt to catch the thistle-down, or played with her flying hair and fluttering ribbon, interpreted in the gestures of her young lithe figure all he felt, but reproduced it unconsciously.

This was, indeed, not England, but the world.

'We're over the edge of everything,' sang Joan, catching at his hand. 'Hold up, Daddy! Hold up!' She tugged him along to join her wild, happy dance. 'You ought to sing. We're over the edge of the world!'

'Above it,' he cried breathlessly. 'We're in the air. Look out, my dear!'

She had suddenly released his hand and sent him spinning with the unaccustomed momentum. Her yellow hair vanished beyond a sea of golden gorse. Her figure melted against it, she was out of sight. 'I'm not a bird yet, at any rate,' he gasped, settling to rest upon a convenient mound and mopping his forehead. 'Not in body, at least. I've got no balance to speak of. I think too much, probably.' He heard her singing somewhere far behind him, and again a lark overhead took up the note and bore it into space.

But with the repose of his creaking muscles and elderly body, the rhythm he had tried to dance now slipped under his ageless and untiring soul. Like a rising wind the Downs were under him and he was up. Seeking a point to settle on, his eye found only strong, subtle lines against the blue, and running along these lines, his spirit was flung forwards with them, upward into limitless space. No peak, no precipice blocked their endless utterance; they flowed, they flew, and Wimble's heart flew with them. The sense of unity, characteristic of airy freedom, invaded his soul triumphantly with its bird's-eye view. He saw life whole beneath him. Perhaps he dozed, perhaps he even slept; at any rate he knew this strange perspective that showed him life, with its huge freight of plodding humanity, rising suddenly into the air.

To rely upon inner, subconscious guidance was to rely upon that portion of his being, that greater portion, which obeyed spontaneously an immense rhythm of the mothering World-Spirit. Thought broke this rhythm; Reason was clever but not wise. The subconscious powers, knowing nothing, yet approached omniscience; enjoyed omnipresence, while still being here. In that state his individuality pooled in sympathy with all others everywhere, tapping a universal wisdom which is available to intuition but not to argument, and is so simple that a child, a bird, may know it easily, singing and dancing its expression naturally. Unerring, infallible, it is the rhythm of divinity, it is reliance upon deity.

This germ of understanding sprouted in his heart, and practice would develop it. He realised himself linked up, not alone with Nature, but with the entire human family, and hence, with Mother. The practice, it was obvious, began with Mother. He must see to it at once. Yet, though clear as crystal in his heart, in his mind it all remained confused, too shy for language, so that he recalled what the railway guard had said, it cannot yet be told, but it can be lived.

His heart flew like a bird through empty space, above all obstacles, above all barriers. There was no detail to enchain attention, nothing to obscure free vision; the soul in him, grand super-bird, took flight. The airy attitude to life became divinely clear and simple, because, with this bird's perspective, he saw life whole. Details that blocked creative energy on earth with fear and difficulty, seemed negligible after all; they were places to take off from. As wings trust carelessly for support upon the universal, ethereal element enveloping them, so could, so must, his will know faith and safety in the immense and powerful rhythms that guide that delicate thrush, the redwing, from Siberia to England every autumn, and steer Sirius unleashed, untroubled, towards his eternal goal. He watched the little wheatears, back from Africa, flitting from perch to perch of tufted grass, soon to leave for their summer in distant Norway. Obedient to this serene and mighty guidance, secure upon these everlasting wings, he saw the bird in humanity open its wings at last. A new reliance upon subconscious inspiration, linking all together, from the butterfly to the angel, flashed through him, air its symbol, wings and flight its emblem. He realised, with an instant's strange intensity, the unity of indivisible air manifested in all forms of life the planet bore.

This undetailed space about him inspired him oddly, it symbolised his dream, the dream that had haunted him since earliest youth. He looked down upon the world beneath him, upon the stretch of years he had flown over, upon the congested streets and houses where men lived, upon the iron conventions and traditions imprisoning their minds from escape into freedom that yet lay so close. The element of earth weighed still heavily upon them; earth builds forms; air, being form-less, offered liberty. He saw these million forms already crumbling; he saw the masses at the upper windows, on the roofs, all looking up. With the coming of air, the day of forms was passing. The ferment, the unrest, the universal questing shone in these upturned eyes. They would not look down again. The vital force had drained out of a thousand forms which have served their day; no past tradition was absolute; they had found it out. Everywhere he saw the emergence of this new spirit, leaving behind it the empty, unsatisfying forms, yearning for fuller self-expression that the unifying ethereal element of air now promised. The roofs were strangely crowded. He saw the myriad figures. He saw that some of them already sang and danced!

Already the new mighty rhythm caught them whirling into space, each soul more and more en rapport with the universal world-soul. Into their hearts, with the lift of wings and a happy bird-like song, it stole subconsciously; the formulae of doctrine which change and shift were giving place to inner experience, and inner experience cannot be destroyed, since it is formless, acknowledging no boundaries, obedient to no creed. Form was dying, life was being born. . . .

He watched the tumbling plover, the sea-gulls grandly sailing, the soaring lark; the floating thistledown went past along the careless wind; he saw his un-thinking daughter's natural, happy dancing, one and all interpreting this message of the air, this promise of liberty that brimmed his deep heart and his uneducated mind. The huge simplicity of the naked Downs made him see existence singularly as a whole; across the open sweep before him the air came sweetly, blowing the tangle of artificial living into easy rhythm and dancing everywhere.

He saw the accidental barriers between creed and sect and nation blown away. A new spiritual unity took their place, a synthetic life, the parts highly specialised, as with birds, yet the whole in perfect harmony. The day of special, exclusive dispensations had disappeared, and this organic spiritual unity, with its new religion of service, lifted the people as with mighty wings.

'Dance on, my child! dance on!' he cried, 'it makes me see things whole!' He watched her light, flying movements against the sea of yellow gorse, the hair like a saffron scarf upon the wind, her radiant face shining and laughing with the blue of endless space behind it. She did not heed his words; she danced away again; she seemed one with the tumbling plover, the sailing sea-birds, and the drifting thistle-down. She danced with the Spring, and the air was in her heart.

The spirit quickened in him as he saw her. His consciousness, he knew, was but a fragment of an immense and deeper consciousness, of limitless scope and powers; this greater self made affirmations to which no mere intellect would dare to set the boundaries. With the air there was a return of joy, belief and wonder into a world that has too long denied all three. Intellect might stand aside a little longer, watching cautiously, like Mother, the flights of intuition, that flashing bird of fire that strikes and vanishes; but science, hitherto destructive chiefly, must enter a new field or be discredited. It must become constructive, it must examine spiritual states. The barrier between the organic and the inorganic was already breached.

'Dance on! My heart flies dancing with you!'

With you! Rather with everything and every one! For he had this curious inspiration, as though all his past condensed now into a single moment, that a new attitude, due to the subliminal consciousness becoming consciously organised with its myriad and mighty powers, was stealing down into the hearts of men from the air. Since its outstanding characteristic was a fuller understanding, a natural sharing, a deep, instinctive sympathy, it involved an actual realisation of spiritual unity that intellect alone has never yet achieved, and never can. It was no flabby, Utopian, idealistic brotherhood he saw, but a practical, co-operative life based upon those greater powers, and upon that completer understanding lying, hid with God, in the subliminal regions of humanity. Experienced hitherto sporadically, only, he saw in what his heart called the promise of the air, their universal acceptance and development. . . . In a second of time, this all flashed into him as he watched the dancing little human figure on the gigantic landscape. And after it, if not actually with it, rose that unaccountable, uneasy, half-terrible emotion of deep-seated pain he had known before the shudder . . . He trembled, tried to sing. Then the gorse pricked him where he lay. He turned to make himself more comfortable. He wriggled. The attempt to sing tickled his throat and he coughed.

He sat up, feeling in his pockets for a pencil and paper. For the first time in his life he felt he must write. 'I must give it out,' he mumbled to himself. 'It's so wonderful, so simple. I must share it. I must tell it to others, to everybody.' He actually made some notes. 'Ah,' he thought, as he read them over a few days later, 'they're no good. I don't quite understand them now, to tell the truth.' He sighed. 'I'm only muddled,' he decided, 'just a Man in the Street bewildered by a touch of inspiration that blew into me!'

He lay watching Joan for a little longer, dancing in the middle distance still. The zest of a bird was in her, the toss, the scamper. Lithe, spinning, sure, her movements interpreted the air far more clearly than his thoughts could compass it in words. Her song came to him with the breeze. He watched her, then waved the packet of sandwiches above his head. He was hungry. They ate their lunch, and spent the rest of the day exploring the great spaces round them.

It was evening when they got home; they heard the random sweetness of the thrush's song among the laurels on the lawn; a nightjar was churning in the dusk beyond; there was a subdued and tiny chattering of the swallows in the eaves. They found Mother among the flower-beds, wearing her big garden-gloves. Wimble took her in his arms and kissed her.

'It's come, Mother, it's come,' he whispered against her cheek. 'And, d'you know? you've been with us all day long.'

She looked up, peaceful and happy, a smell of garden earth about her, and the glow of the sunset in her eyes. 'Have I really, Joe dear?' she said. 'How lovely!' And then she added: 'I believe it is; yes, I believe it is.'

Next morning Wimble woke very, very early, close upon three o'clock. He peered out of the window a moment. The dawn, he saw with a happy sigh of wonder, was just beginning to break. The gleam of light fell upon Mother's face; and the singing of a lark high up in the clearing air came to him. At the same moment Mother moved in her bed close by; her heavy breathing was interrupted. He listened. She was talking in her sleep, though the words were indistinguishable. He waited, thinking she might get up and walk. Her eyes, however, did not open; she lay still again. He slipped over to tuck the blankets more securely round her. 'Bless her!' he thought. 'She's asleep! Her surface consciousness is merged with her deep, safe, wise subconsciousness' And his thought broke off abruptly. It had suddenly occurred to him that the sleep-walker and the migrating bird both found their way unerringly in the darkness, both obedient to inner guidance. He stood still an instant, looking down upon her face in the pale morning light.

'Who, what guides the redwing over hills, and vales, and seas?' he whispered. 'Who, what guides the sleep-walker amid the intricacies of Maple furniture?' He chuckled to himself. It was odd how the comic Aquarian lecture cropped up in his memory like this once more.

He bent down and kissed her lightly on the cheek, then went back to bed. Mother still mumbled in her sleep 'Flow, fly, flow,' he seemed to catch, 'it's coming, coming . . .'

'It's the bird returning to her heart,' he whispered to himself. Deep down inside her being something sang; outside, the carolling of the lark continued, blithe and joyous in the breaking dawn. As he fell asleep, the two sounds were so curiously mingled that they seemed almost indistinguishable. . . .

Algernon Blackwood – A Short Biography

Algernon Blackwood (1869-1951) was one of the most prolific English writers of the twentieth century across short stories, novels and plays. His passion for the supernatural and for ghost stories often made readers and critics to compare him to M. R. James and Sheridan Le Fanu. Some even argue that he had a more sophisticated style and that a more artistic touch marked his extraordinary storytelling. Today, much of his excellent fiction remains out of print and undiscovered by the wide public.

Algernon Blackwood was born in on March 14th 1869 in Shooter's Hill, now part of modern day South East London, to an upper middle-class family who led a religious life. His mother was a widowed Duchess and his father was her second husband. Biographers believe that Algernon started to be interested in subjects related to the paranormal and the supernatural at an early age, being influenced by the kind of life his parents were living as new converts to Calvinism. His father, who was a post office administrator, sent him to be educated at Wellington College. However, his fascination with "weird" stories only grew stronger and he started to read on Oriental philosophies, mysticism and occultism. Later, his interests made him join the renowned The Ghost Club which had earlier been joined by other important writers such as Arthur Conan Doyle and William Butler Yeats.

It was hence that Algernon Blackwood started to consider writing on the subject of the supernatural and his writings took various forms ranging from the ghost story and children's stories to plays and long novels. However, in addition to displaying his wide knowledge related to subjects such as mysticism, hypnotism and ghosts, Blackwood's writings were also enriched by his long and diversified life experience. In fact, after leaving university and visiting parts of Europe, mainly Switzerland, the young writer was sent to the new continent. He settled in Canada and then in the United States where he occupied numerous different jobs and extended his comprehension of life and people. He worked as a farmer, a bartender, a secretary, a journalist and a reporter, and a teacher. This enriching experience was not very successful on the financial level, though, and he eventually had to return to his home land.

It was only when he came back to England that Blackwood started to give his writing activities more importance. It all started when two of his supernatural stories were published in the Pall Mall Magazine. They were entitled "A Haunted Island" (1906) and "A Case of Eavesdropping" (1900) and dealt with weird apparition. Meanwhile, the young writer kept on travelling and enriching his experience and imagination, meeting new people and visiting new places. Blackwood's name started to be associated with supernatural fiction among the literary circles of the age as more of his highly-entertaining stories were published. In 1906, his first volume was published under the title *The Empty House and Other Ghost Stories* and realized considerable success. In addition to the other strange accounts related in the volume, the eponymous story centers around the then classic theme of the haunted house and follows the heroes who accept a challenge to spend a night inside the house. It is believed that most of these stories were based on the author's personal experiences.

While being rather unsuccessful with non-fiction and journalistic reports, Blackwood's rise to fame with his ghost stories was phenomenal. More collections of short and ghost stories followed, including *The Listener and Other Stories* (1907) and *John Silence: Physician Extraordinary* (1908), which were flavored by the introduction of a detective tone. When Blackwood's stories achieved an outstanding success, publishers encouraged him to produce more and he was invited by radio and television to retell his stories, which helped popularize his works and familiarize his name. During the same period, Blackwood also published a number of stories for children which do not all draw on the supernatural tradition. These included a Victorian love story entitled "The Story of Karl Ott," published in the *Pall Mall Magazine* in 1896. In 1910, there was also the publication of a collection of stories for children under the title *The Lost Valley and Other Stories*. With the outbreak of the First World War, Blackwood was assigned a responsibility with the British intelligence and engaged in writing propaganda to support his country's war efforts.

While developing a life-time personal interest in occultism and the metaphysical, Blackwood often expressed implicit criticism of organized religion and openly criticized churchman at times. For instance, this can be perceived in one of his short stories entitled "An Egyptian Hornet" published in 1915. The story juxtaposes the behavior of two Englishmen staying in the same hotel in Egypt. The one is a priest who is there to give masses to the English living in Egypt and the second is an irreligious drunkard who never hides his contempt for parsons. By the end of the story, the hypocrisy and cowardice of the priest and the honesty and bravery of his adversary are unveiled by the little insect of the title. What is particularly entertaining in the narrative, however, is the way Blackwood minutely and figuratively describes the Egyptian wasp:

The word has an angry, malignant sound that brings the idea of attack vividly into the mind. There is a vicious sting about it somewhere - even a foreigner, ignorant of the meaning, must feel it. A hornet is wicked; it darts and stabs; it pierces, aiming without provocation for the face and eyes. The name suggests a metallic droning of evil wings, fierce flight, and poisonous assault. Though black and yellow, it sounds scarlet. There is blood in it. A striped tiger of the air in concentrated form! There is no escape - if it attacks.

The 1910s was also the period when Blackwood started to be interested in writing novels. The latter form offered him the opportunity to develop more serious ideas about the paranormal world and to explore the relationship between man and metaphysical powers. This manifests, for instance, in one of his most important novels entitled *The Centaur* published in 1911. Many critics and biographers argue that Blackwood's oeuvre and the themes developed in them reflect the author's own personality and experience. This was also confirmed in the plays that he started to write at a later stage. Among his most popular plays, one can probably mention *The Starlight Express* (1915) which was co-authored by Violet Pearn and which was actually an adaptation of an earlier novel by Blackwood entitled *A Prisoner in Fairyland*. Blackwood also wrote other plays and in 1927 another influential collection of short stories was published under the title *The Dance of Death and Other Tales*.

Apart from a sole autobiography that Blackwood wrote earlier in his life and entitled *Episodes before Thirty* (1923), a number of critical works dealt with his life and works. These included a biography by the British editor and bibliographer Mike Ashley. The volume is entitled *Algernon Blackwood: An Extraordinary Life* (2001). The name of Blackwood also appeared in H. P. Lovecraft's seminal and foundational work on horror fiction, "Supernatural Horror in Literature" in which the American horror writer and critic hails him as one of the "masters". Lovecraft mainly showed a particular fascination with Blackwood's tale entitled "The Willows" which he considered as an ultimate masterpiece.

Towards his last years, Blackwood published *The Doll and One Other* which was also a runaway success. The eponymous story deals with the motif of the supernaturally malignant little doll, a motif that has incessantly kept on returning after Blackwood. In 1949, Blackwood was made a Commander of the Order of the British Empire which was an official recognition of his literary merits as well as of the services he presented to the British nation during the First World War. Other tales of sorceries and magic were anthologized following Blackwood's death. Having spent a very hectic life, full of travelling and explorations of the natural and the supernatural, Algernon Blackwood died on December 10th, 1951 after a series of strokes. His ashes were sprinkled on Mount Saanenmoser in Switzerland, a place that the writer was fond of and that he had visited on many an occasion. Literary scholars and critics recognized the merits of Algernon Blackwood as a major contributor to horror fiction, ghost stories and the Gothic genre. He was, indeed, somebody who dedicated his whole life to the quest of the supernatural and had always understood that what is hidden and kept beyond natural consciousness should be more pertinently explored through the arts and the imagination. As he was to write "My fundamental interest, I suppose, is signs and proofs of other powers that lie hidden in us all; the extension, in other words, of human faculty. So many of my stories, therefore, deal with extension of consciousness; speculative and imaginative treatment of possibilities outside our normal range of consciousness. ... Also, all that happens in our universe is *natural*; under Law; but an extension of our so limited normal consciousness can reveal new, extra-ordinary powers etc., and the word "supernatural" seems the best word for treating these in fiction. I believe it possible for our consciousness to change and grow, and that with this change we may become aware of a new universe. A "change" in consciousness, in its type, I mean, is something more than a mere extension of what we already possess and know.

Algernon Blackwood - A Concise Bibliography

Novels

Jimbo: A Fantasy (1909)

The Education of Uncle Paul (1909)

The Human Chord (1910)

The Centaur (1911)

A Prisoner in Fairyland (1913)

The Extra Day (1915)

Julius LeVallon (1916)

The Wave (1916)

The Promise of Air (1918)

The Garden of Survival (1918)

The Bright Messenger (1921)

Dudley & Gilderoy: A Nonsense (1929)

Children's Novels:

Sambo and Snitch (1927)

The Fruit Stoners: Being the Adventures of Maria Among the Fruit Stoners (1934)

Plays

The Starlight Express (1915), coauthored with Violet Pearn; incidental music by Edward Elgar; based on Blackwood's 1913 novel A Prisoner in Fairyland

Karma a reincarnation play in prologue epilogue and three acts (1918), coauthored with Violet Pearn;

The Crossing (1920a), coauthored with Bertram Forsyth; based on Blackwood's 1913 short story "Transition"

Through the Crack (1920b), coauthored with Violet Pearn; based on Blackwood's 1909 novel The Education of Uncle Paul and 1915 novel The Extra Day

White Magic (1921a), coauthored with Bertram Forsyth

The Halfway House (1921b), coauthored with Elaine Ainley

Max Hensig (1929), coauthored with Frederick Kinsey Peile; based on Blackwood's 1907 short story "Max Hensig — Bacteriologist and Murderer"

Short Story Collections

The Empty House and Other Ghost Stories (1906)

The Listener and Other Stories (1907)

John Silence (1908)

The Lost Valley and Other Stories (1910)

Pan's Garden: a Volume of Nature Stories (1912)

Ten Minute Stories (1914)

Incredible Adventures (1914)

Day and Night Stories (1917)

Wolves of God, and Other Fey Stories (1921) coauthored with Wilfred Wilson

Tongues of Fire and Other Sketches (1924)

Ancient Sorceries and Other Tales (1927)

The Dance of Death and Other Tales (1927)

Strange Stories (1929) selections from previous Blackwood collections

Short Stories of To-Day & Yesterday (1930); selections from previous Blackwood collections

The Willows and Other Queer Tales (1932); selections from previous Blackwood collections

Shocks (1935)

The Tales of Algernon Blackwood (1938); selections from previous Blackwood collections

Selected Tales of Algernon Blackwood (1942); selections from previous Blackwood collections.

Selected Short Stories of Algernon Blackwood (1945); selections from previous Blackwood collections

The Doll and One Other (1946)

Tales of the Uncanny and Supernatural (1949); selections from previous Blackwood collections

In the Realm of Terror (1957); selections from previous Blackwood collections

www.ingramcontent.com/pod-product-compliance
Lightning Source LLC
Chambersburg PA
CBHW051308170626
46809CB00004B/1806